# TELL ME ABOUT

# THE HUMAN BODY

An Hachette UK Company
www.hachette.co.uk

First published in Great Britain in 2016 by Chancellor Press,
a division of Octopus Publishing Group Ltd
Carmelite House, 50 Victoria Embankment, London EC4Y 0DZ
www.octopusbooks.co.uk

Edited and designed by Anna Southgate and Leah Germann

ISBN 978-0-7537-3032-4

A CIP catalogue record for this book is available from the British Library

Printed and bound in China

10 9 8 7 6 5 4 3 2 1

Publisher: Lucy Pessell
Design Manager: Megan van Staden
Editor: Natalie Bradley
Production Controller: Sarah Kulasek-Boyd

## UPDATED & REVISED

# TELL ME ABOUT ᴛʜᴇ HUMAN BODY

## ANSWERS TO HUNDREDS OF FASCINATING QUESTIONS

CHANCELLOR
PRESS

# CONTENTS

# THE BRAIN AND
# THE NERVOUS SYSTEM

# CONTENTS

# WHAT ARE THE AREAS OF THE BRAIN CALLED?

Our brains have five distinct areas, each of which controls specific activities that we do from day to day. The cerebrum – a big, wrinkled dome that covers most of the top of the brain – is the part that controls thought. It has a thin outer layer of 'grey matter', which is mainly nerve cells, covering an inner mass of 'white matter', chiefly nerve fibres.

The other parts of the brain are the cerebellum, which carries out detailed control of muscles; the thalamus, which helps to sort and process information from four of the senses (eyes, ears, tongue, skin); the hypothalamus, which regulates temperature and controls thirst, hunger and sleep; and the brain stem – the base of the brain, which contains the main 'life support' areas for heartbeat, breathing, blood pressure and control of digestion. Its lower end merges into the top of the spinal cord.

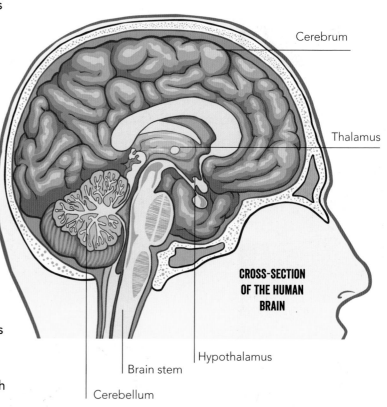

Cerebrum

Thalamus

**CROSS-SECTION OF THE HUMAN BRAIN**

Hypothalamus

Brain stem

Cerebellum

**THE CEREBRUM MAKES UP MORE THAN FOUR-FIFTHS OF THE WHOLE BRAIN!**

**• FACT FILE •**

Even when asleep, the brain is just as active as it is when awake, and sends nerve messages around itself. Young children often take naps during the day.

# HOW IS THE
# CEREBRUM ORGANIZED?

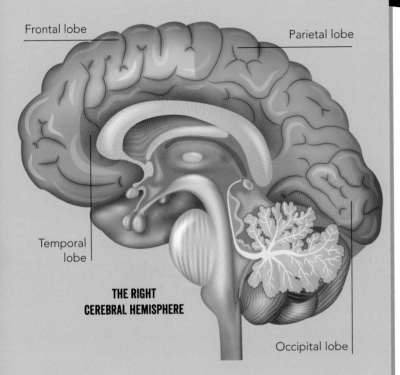

Frontal lobe

Parietal lobe

Temporal lobe

**THE RIGHT CEREBRAL HEMISPHERE**

Occipital lobe

• **FACT FILE** •

Shivering is governed by four mechanisms. The hypothalamus, at the base of the brain, senses that the temperature is too low and sends messages to the thyroid gland, telling it to speed up the metabolic rate. The body muscles then alternately contract and relax rapidly, thus producing heat. The nerves then send messages to the skin and the skin pores narrow, ensuring that the heat is conserved within the body.

The cerebrum is in the brain and makes up about 85 per cent of its weight. A large groove called the longitudinal fissure divides the cerebrum into halves called the left cerebral hemisphere and the right cerebral hemisphere. The hemispheres are connected by bundles of nerves, the largest of which is the corpus callosum. Each hemisphere, in turn, is divided into four lobes. Each lobe has the same name as the bone of the skull that lies above it. The lobes are the frontal lobe, at the front; the temporal lobe, at the lower side; the parietal lobe, in the middle; and the occipital lobe, at the rear.

# WHAT ARE THE MAIN FUNCTIONS OF THE BRAIN?

The brain is the body's control centre. It keeps the body working smoothly and it looks after thoughts, feelings and memory. Different parts of the brain have different jobs to do. The largest part is called the cerebrum, or forebrain. It looks like a huge half-walnut. The cerebrum's main job is to sort out and respond to messages sent to it from the senses. It also stores information, as memory, and it thinks.

Messages from the senses are managed by the cerebrum's sensory area, while the motor area controls the muscles. Thinking, memory and speech are managed by the parts known as the association areas. The cerebellum is below the cerebrum. It works with the cerebrum's motor area to ensure that the muscles function smoothly.

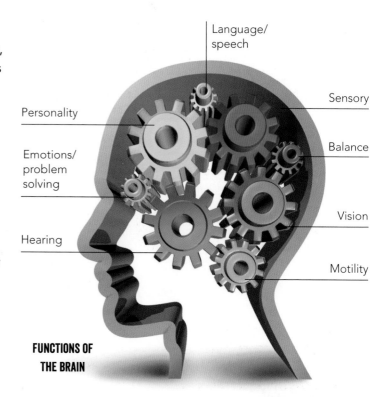

Language/speech

Sensory

Balance

Vision

Motility

Personality

Emotions/problem solving

Hearing

**FUNCTIONS OF THE BRAIN**

**FACT FILE**

Although we have invented computers that can work out millions of different things in seconds, our brains can still outwork and outsmart them! Our brains control our bodies by sending out billions of tiny electrical signals every second.

**?**

**DID YOU KNOW THAT THE CEREBRUM IS MORE DEVELOPED IN HUMANS THAN IN ANY OTHER ANIMAL?**

# HOW DOES MEMORY WORK?

Prefrontal cortex

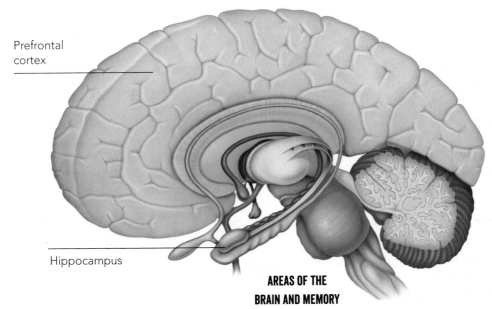

Hippocampus

**AREAS OF THE BRAIN AND MEMORY**

Short-term memory takes place in the prefrontal cortex, along with thought; long-term memory takes place in the hippocampus.

**THE ADULT BRAIN CAN MEMORIZE TENS OF THOUSANDS OF WORDS!**

Memory is the ability to store things that you experience and learn, ready for use in the future. Some things are remembered easily, such as dramatic events in your life. However, more ordinary things need to be rehearsed in the mind several times before they 'stick'.

There are different ways of storing memory:

- Sensory memory: This is very brief. It tells you what is happening around you and allows you to move without bumping into things.

- Short-term memory: This lasts for only about 30 seconds. It allows you to remember a phone number and dial it, but after a minute or so it will vanish.

- Long-term memory: This is for things that you have carefully memorized and learned.

**• FACT FILE •**

The sense of smell is closely linked with retrieving memories. Often a smell, like the burning of a bonfire, can suddenly trigger a memory from many years ago.

# WHAT IS THE AUTONOMIC NERVOUS SYSTEM?

**THE AUTONOMIC NERVOUS SYSTEM**

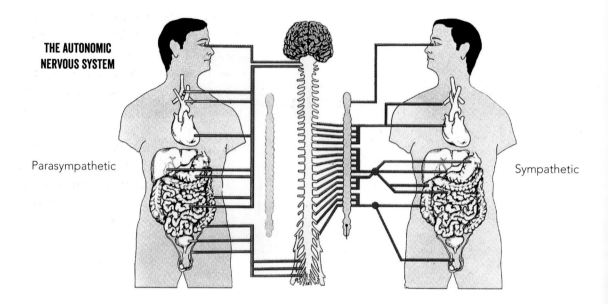

Parasympathetic

Sympathetic

The autonomic nervous system regulates such automatic bodily processes as breathing and digestion without conscious control by the brain. This constant regulation enables the body to maintain a stable internal environment. The autonomic nervous system has two parts, the sympathetic and the parasympathetic system. The parasympathetic nerves tend to make the body calm and relaxed, and slow down processes such as digestion and heartbeat. The sympathetic nerves speed up all these processes and activities, so that the body is ready to spring into action. Between them, these two sets of nerves fine-tune the body's internal conditions.

## • FACT FILE •

The autonomic system is controlled by an area of the brain called the hypothalamus (shown here in blue). This receives information about any variations in your body.

# HOW ARE MESSAGES PASSED THROUGH THE NERVOUS SYSTEM?

Nerve impulses that pass through the nervous system are able to jump from one neurone to the next. Inside the nerve fibre, the nerve impulse travels as an electrical signal. When it reaches the end of the long fibre, it jumps across to the next neurone by means of a chemical transmitter. This chemical is released from the branched ends of the fibre. As this transmitter substance contacts the next neurone, it starts another nerve impulse. This whole process is very fast.

**NERVE IMPULSES TRAVEL ALONG THE LARGEST NERVE FIBRES AT 90M (295FT) PER SECOND!**

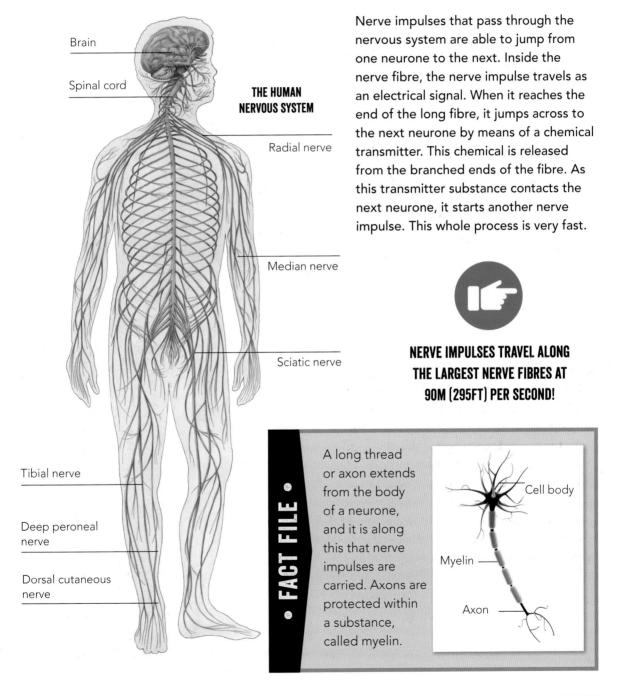

Brain

Spinal cord

**THE HUMAN NERVOUS SYSTEM**

Radial nerve

Median nerve

Sciatic nerve

Tibial nerve

Deep peroneal nerve

Dorsal cutaneous nerve

## FACT FILE

A long thread or axon extends from the body of a neurone, and it is along this that nerve impulses are carried. Axons are protected within a substance, called myelin.

Cell body

Myelin

Axon

# HOW DO NERVE IMPULSES WORK?

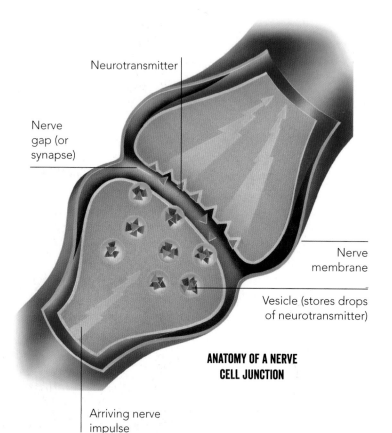

Neurotransmitter

Nerve gap (or synapse)

Nerve membrane

Vesicle (stores drops of neurotransmitter)

**ANATOMY OF A NERVE CELL JUNCTION**

Arriving nerve impulse

A nerve impulse is like a very simple message: either 'on' or 'off'. Because there are so many neurones that are connected to one another, this simple signal is enough to carry the most complicated messages throughout the whole of the body's nervous system. As a nerve impulse arrives at the junction between two nerve cells, it is carried across the gap or synapse by chemicals called neurotransmitters. These neurotransmitters contact sensitive areas in the next nerve cell, and the nerve impulse is carried along.

**Messages are sent to the brain from different parts of the body and back again through the nerves.**

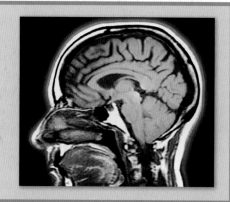

# WHICH NERVE IN THE BODY IS THE THICKEST?

The thickest nerve in the human body is the sciatic nerve, located in the hip and upper thigh. It is about the width of its owner's thumb. This is thicker than the spinal cord, which is usually the width of its owner's little finger.

Our nerve systems control our every movement and action, and every process that happens inside the body. Your nervous system is made up of your brain, spinal cord and nerves. It works by sending tiny electrical signals called nerve impulses. Millions of these travel around the body and brain every second, like the busiest computer network. When you hurt a finger you probably feel the touch first, and then the pain starts a moment later. This is because the signals about touch travel faster along the nerves than the signals about pain.

There are two main nervous systems within the body. The central nervous system is the brain's main control centre. It sends nerve impulses to the rest of the body using the peripheral nervous system. We have conscious control over the central and peripheral nervous systems.

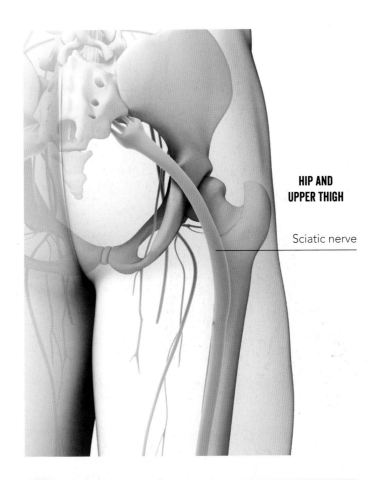

**HIP AND UPPER THIGH**

Sciatic nerve

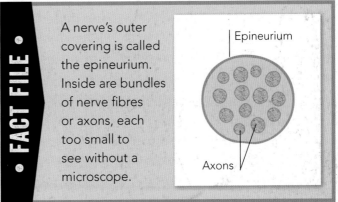

**FACT FILE**

A nerve's outer covering is called the epineurium. Inside are bundles of nerve fibres or axons, each too small to see without a microscope.

Epineurium

Axons

# WHAT CONTROLS OUR BALANCE?

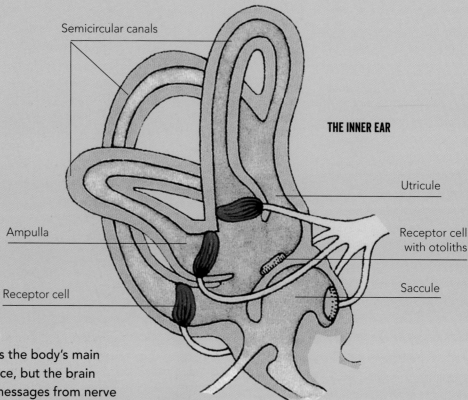

Semicircular canals

THE INNER EAR

Utricule

Ampulla

Receptor cell with otoliths

Receptor cell

Saccule

The inner ear is the body's main organ of balance, but the brain also receives messages from nerve endings in the neck, back, leg and feet muscles. The brain sifts all this information and sends messages back to the muscles, allowing us to perform incredible feats of balance such as ice-skating or gymnastics. Near the cochlea are fluid-filled tubes – the semicircular canals. As your head moves about, the fluid inside each canal swishes to and fro. When the body moves, the fluid causes hairs in a jelly-like mass to bend. These are connected to the vestibular nerve, which alerts the brain to re-balance the body.

## • FACT FILE •

You feel dizzy after you spin round and round because the liquid in your ears is still swirling about when you stop, and your brain can't tell where you're going! If you watch a dancer spin round, you will see that their head does not move continuously.

# WHAT CONTROLS
# OUR TEMPERATURE?

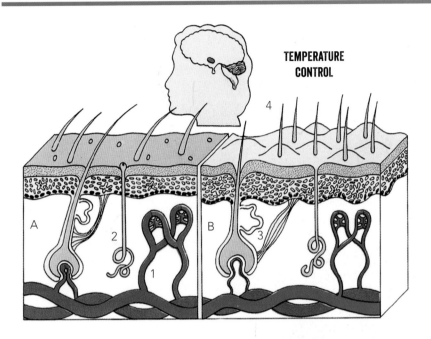

TEMPERATURE
CONTROL

The name for 'constancy of the internal environment' is homeostasis. The body must regulate many body systems and processes to keep inner conditions stable. The temperature nucleus in the hypothalamus controls heat loss and production by the body through the skin. Overheating (A) causes an increased blood flow from the blood vessels (1), to radiate heat and causes sweating through the sweat glands (2), to lose heat. A fall in body temperature (B) constricts the surface blood vessels, stops sweating and makes the erector muscles (3) contract, causing the hairs (4) to stand on end, trapping air as an insulating layer. Additional heat can be produced by shivering.

DID YOU KNOW THAT HUMANS HAVE A 'NORMAL' BODY TEMPERATURE OF 37°C (98.6°F)?

## • FACT FILE •

Body movements can also be homeostatic. A person feeling too hot may spread out arms and legs to increase heat loss; a person feeling too cold curls up to reduce the areas of the body losing warmth.

# WHEN DOES OUR SENSE OF TOUCH ALERT THE BRAIN TO DANGER?

Close your eyes and touch something – your clothes, a table, a car or even your own skin. Stroke it gently. What does it feel like? Is it hard or soft, hot or cold? The surface may be smooth, bumpy, gritty, furry or hairy. It could be dry, moist, or slimy. Your skin continuously passes huge amounts of information to the brain. It monitors touch, pain, temperature and other factors that tell the brain exactly how the body is being affected by its environment. Without this constant flow of information, you would keep injuring yourself accidentally, which is what happens in some rare diseases where the skin senses are lost.

Senses in the skin are measured by tiny receptors at the ends of nerves. There are several different types of receptor. Each type can detect only one kind of sensation, such as pain, temperature, pressure, touch and so on.

**SENSING DANGER**

Receptors in the skin send messages to the brain.

Your skin is in constant contact with the outside world, sending messages to your brain.

# WHEN DO WE USE OUR BRAIN TO SMELL?

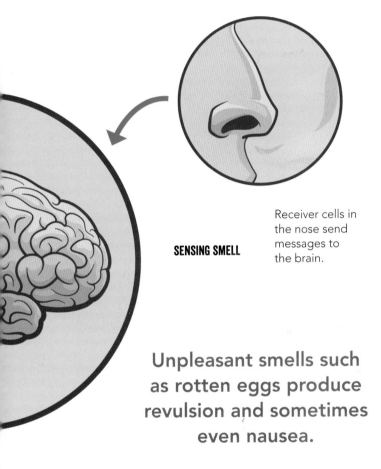

**SENSING SMELL**

Receiver cells in the nose send messages to the brain.

## • FACT FILE •

Aromatherapy is the art of using the perfumed essential oils of plants to treat the body and mind. The perfume passes over the nerve cells in the nasal passage and a message is sent to the brain.

Unpleasant smells such as rotten eggs produce revulsion and sometimes even nausea.

The part of the brain that analyzes messages coming from the receiver cells in the nose is closely connected with the limbic system, that part of the brain that deals with emotions, moods and memory. It is called the primitive brain, sometimes even the 'smelling brain'. The connection explains why smells are richly supplied with emotional significance. The smell of fresh rain on a summer's day usually makes people feel happy and invigorated, and it may also evoke happy memories. The smell of fresh-baked bread may bring on instant pangs of hunger, while the scent of perfume may remind you of a loved one. Certain smells will bring memories of long forgotten special occasions flooding back. This is because the areas of the brain that process memories are also closely linked to the limbic system.

# WHY DO WE GET THIRSTY?

Can you imagine how it would feel to be thirsty for days? If a human being has absolutely nothing to drink for five to six days, he will die. Feeling thirsty is simply our body's way of telling us to replenish its liquid supply.

The reason for this thirst is caused by a change in the salt content of our blood. There is a certain normal amount of salt and water in our blood. When this ratio changes and we have more salt in relation to water in our blood, thirst results.

There is a part of our brain called the 'thirst centre'. It responds to the amount of salt in our blood. When there is a change, it sends messages to the back of the throat. From there, messages go to the brain, and it is this combination of feelings that makes us say we are thirsty.

## FACT FILE

Onions send out an irritating substance when we chop them. The onion has an oil containing sulphur, which not only gives it its sharp odour, but it also irritates the eye. The eye reacts by blinking and producing tears to wash it away. That is why we cry when we chop onions.

**DID YOU KNOW THAT YOUR BODY IS ABOUT 60% WATER?**

# WHY DO WE GET HUNGRY?

Have you ever wondered how your brain gets the message that makes you feel hungry?

Hunger begins when certain nutritive materials are missing in the blood. When the blood vessels lack these materials, a message is sent to a part of the brain that is called the 'hunger centre'. This hunger centre works like a brake on the stomach and the intestine. As long as the blood has sufficient food, the hunger centre slows up the action of the stomach and the intestine. When the food is missing from the blood, the hunger centre makes the stomach and intestine more active. That is why when you're hungry, you can often hear your stomach rumbling.

When we are hungry, our body doesn't crave any special kind of food it just wants nourishment. It depends on the individual how long we can actually live without food. A very calm person can live longer than an excitable one because the protein stored up in their body is used up more slowly.

## • FACT FILE •

Eggs are an extremely good form of protein, which is vital for the building up and repair of muscles. Milk and dairy products are another really good source of protein.

Most people believe that hunger relates to having an empty stomach, but this is not true.

# WHY DO
# WE DREAM?

All our dreams have something to do with our emotions, fears, longings, wishes, needs and memories. But something on the 'outside' may influence what we dream. If you are hungry, tired, or cold, your dreams may well include these feelings. If the covers have slipped off your bed, you may dream you are on an iceberg. There are people called psychoanalysts who have made a special study of why people dream. They believe that dreams are expressions of wishes that didn't come true. In other words, a dream is a way of having your wish fulfilled. During sleep, according to this theory, our inhibitions are also asleep.

**?** DID YOU KNOW THAT DURING A NIGHT'S SLEEP, A PERSON MAY CHANGE POSITION AS MANY AS 40 TIMES AND HAVE 5 DREAMS?

# WHY DO WE AWAKEN FROM SLEEP?

Everybody has strange experiences with sleep. Sometimes we can't wait to go to sleep and other times we just can't seem to get to sleep. What actually wakes us up is something that scientists find hard to explain.

When we go about thinking and seeing and feeling and carrying on mental activities of all sorts, we use up a lot of energy. So the brain and other nerve centres need a rest. Sleep clears away our tiredness and when we wake up we feel rested.

The most probable reason is that while we are asleep our body still feels hungry, cold or even damp, or we may experience an emotion such as fear. These feelings stimulate our brain and cause us to wake up.

Of course we may wake up simply because we have had enough sleep!

# WHY ARE SOME PEOPLE LEFT-HANDED?

Many of the greatest geniuses have been left-handed. Leonardo da Vinci and Michelangelo – two of the greatest sculptors of all time – were both left-handed.

About four per cent of the population is left-handed. The brain has a right half and a left half and these two do not function in the same way. It is believed that the left half of the brain is predominant over the right half. As the left half of the brain predominates, the right half of the body is more skilled and better able to do things. We read, write, speak and work with the left half of our brain. And this, of course, makes most of us right-handed too. But in the case of left-handed people, it works the other way around. The right half of the brain is predominant, and such a person works best with the left side of their body.

# WHY CAN WE BALANCE ON TWO LEGS?

Just being able to stand up or to walk is one of the most amazing tricks it is possible to learn. When you stand still, you are performing a constant act of balancing. You change from one leg to the other, you use pressure on your joints, and your muscles tell your body to go this way and that way. In walking, we not only use our balancing trick, but we also make use of two natural forces to help us. The first is air pressure. Our thighbone fits into the socket of the hip joint so snugly that it forms a kind of vacuum. The air pressure on our legs helps keep it there securely. This air pressure also makes the leg hang from the body as if it had very little weight. The second natural force we use in walking is the pull of the Earth's gravity. When we raise our leg, the Earth pulls it down again.

**IT TAKES THE WORK OF ABOUT 300 MUSCLES JUST TO BALANCE WHEN STANDING STILL!**

# THE SKELETON, JOINTS AND MUSCLES

# CONTENTS

# WHY DO
# WE HAVE A SKELETON?

A skeleton is made up of a network of bones. Bones provide a framework that holds the whole body together. Without a skeleton, we would not be supported and would simply flop about like rag dolls. This would mean that we would not be able to move about. The skeleton also gives protection to delicate organs in our bodies such as the brain, heart and lungs. It acts as a support to all the soft parts of the body. The skeleton also provides a system of levers that the muscles can work on, enabling us to carry out all our movements.

## • FACT FILE •

There are 206 bones in the average body. However, there are a few people who have more, such as an extra pair of ribs, making 13 pairs instead of 12 and therefore 208 bones in total. At birth, a baby has 300 bones, but 94 join together in early childhood.

THE HUMAN HAND ALONE CONTAINS AN IMPRESSIVE 27 BONES!

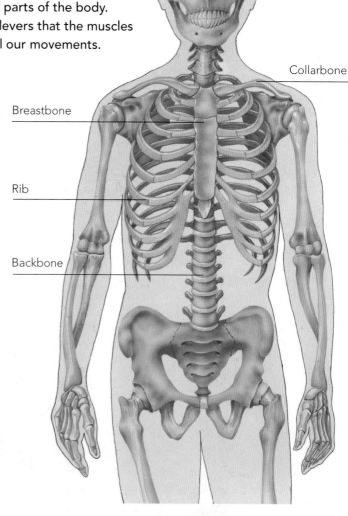

Skull

Collarbone

Breastbone

Rib

Backbone

THE HUMAN SKELETON

# WHAT IS
# BONE MADE FROM?

A typical bone is actually made of two types of bony tissue. On the outside is a type of 'skin' called the periosteum. Below this is a thin layer of thick, dense, 'solid' bone. It is known as hard or compact bony tissue. Inside this, and forming the bulk of the middle of the bone, is a different bony tissue, more like a sponge or honeycomb. It has gaps and spaces, and it is called spongy, or alveolar, bony tissue. It is much lighter than the outer compact bone, and the spaces are filled with blood vessels, and jelly-like bone marrow for making new blood cells.

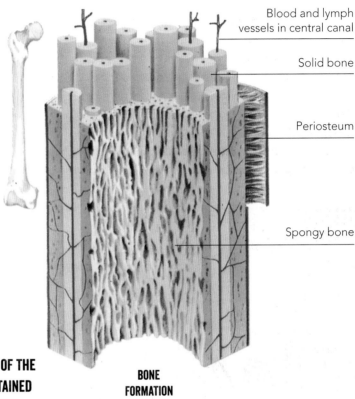

Blood and lymph vessels in central canal

Solid bone

Periosteum

Spongy bone

**BONE FORMATION**

**MORE THAN 99 PER CENT OF THE BODY'S CALCIUM IS CONTAINED IN THE BONES AND TEETH!**

# WHICH BONES MAKE UP THE SPINE?

The spine is made up of a column of bones called vertebrae. The spine is the part of the skeleton that extends down the middle of the back. The spine plays an important role in posture and movement, and it also protects the spinal cord. The human spine consists of 33 vertebrae, but some of them grow together in adults. There are 7 cervical (neck), 12 thoracic (chest region), 5 lumbar (lower back), 5 sacral (hip region) and 4 coccygeal (tailbone region) vertebrae. The vertebrae are held in place by muscles and strong connective tissue called ligaments. Most vertebrae have fibrous intervertebral discs between them to absorb shock and enable the spine to bend. The spine normally has a slight natural curve.

**The spine is also called the spinal column, vertebral column or backbone.**

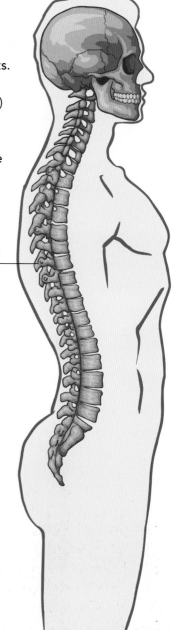

Vertebrae

## • FACT FILE •

Many people get backache. Sometimes the intervertebral disc, the tissue that lies between the vertebrae, sticks out and presses on nerves. This condition is called a slipped disc (shown here in red). It can cause severe pain in the lower back, thighs and legs.

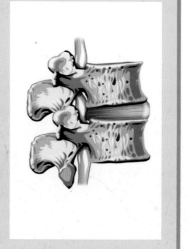

# WHERE IS
# YOUR OCCIPITAL BONE?

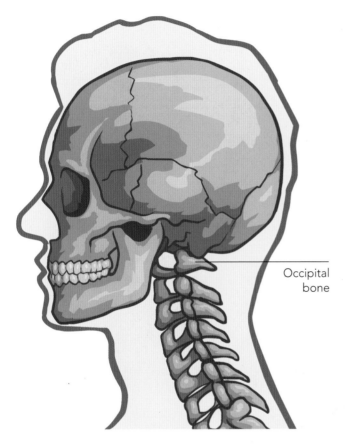

Occipital bone

A system of muscles and tendons connects the head to the spinal column, the collarbone and the shoulder blades. These muscles and tendons control the movement of the head. The occipital bone forms the back of the skull. This bone rests on the spinal column and forms a joint on which the head moves. Most of the weight of the head is in front of the occipital bone, and the head is held in an erect position by muscles in the neck. When a person becomes sleepy, these muscles relax and the head falls forward. Other large bones of the head include the maxilla, the mandible, and the parietal, frontal, sphenoid and temporal bones.

## The occipital bone is one of eight bones that make up the cranium.

# WHERE ARE THE METACARPALS?

The metacarpals are bones in the human hand. The hand consists of the carpals (wrist bones), the metacarpals (palm bones) and the phalanges (four fingers and thumb). There are 27 bones in the hand. Eight carpal bones make up the wrist. They are arranged roughly in two rows. In the row nearest the forearm, starting from the thumb side, are the scaphoid, lunate, triquetrum and pisiform bones. In the second row are the trapezium, trapezoid, capitate and hamate bones. Five long metacarpal bones make up the palm. They connect the wrist with the fingers and thumb. Each of the four fingers contains three slender phalanges, while the thumb contains only two phalanges.

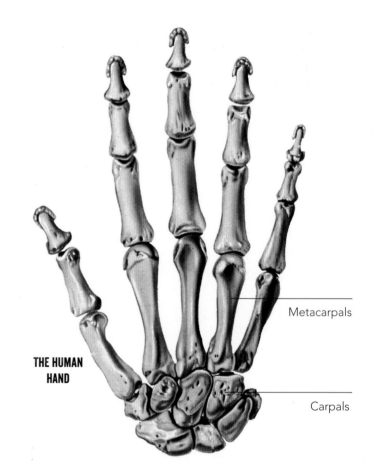

**THE HUMAN HAND**

Metacarpals

Carpals

## FACT FILE

The human foot has 26 bones in total. These are the seven tarsals, or anklebones; the five metatarsals, or instep bones; and the 14 phalanges, or toe bones.

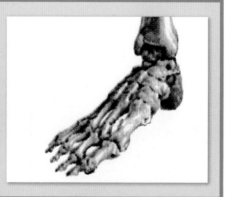

# WHERE IS THE HUMERUS BONE?

The humerus bone is in the arm. The elbow is the joint that connects a person's upper arm with the forearm. The humerus (the bone of the upper arm) and the radius and ulna (the bones of the forearm) meet at the elbow. The three bone connections form three smaller joints within the elbow joint. These smaller joints permit certain movements. The humerus–ulna joint and the humerus–radius joint allow a person to bend the forearm up and down. The radius–ulna joint and the humerus–radius joint permit a person to rotate the forearm and to turn the palm of the hand up and down. A capsule of tough connective tissue surrounds the elbow joint. This capsule and several ligaments hold the bones in place.

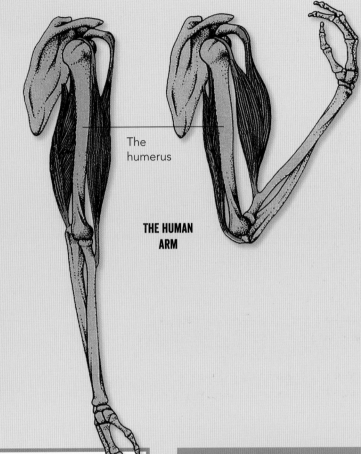

The humerus

**THE HUMAN ARM**

## FACT FILE

Excessive or violent twisting of the forearm may injure the elbow ligaments, capsule or tendons. One such injury, sometimes called tennis elbow, often results from playing tennis.

**?**

DID YOU KNOW THAT THE HUMERUS IS THE ARM'S LARGEST BONE? IT ALSO HAPPENS TO BE THE ONLY BONE IN THE UPPER ARM.

# WHICH BONES FORM YOUR PELVIS?

Two big, symmetrical hipbones form the pelvis. These bones join in front to form the pubic symphysis. In the back, they form a strong union with the sacrum.

Each hipbone in an adult appears to be one solid bone, but it is formed by three bones; the ilium, the ischium and the pubis, that unite as the body matures. The ilium is the broad, flat bone you feel when you rest your hand on your hip. When you sit down, much of your weight rests on the ischium. The pelvis is the bony structure that supports the lower abdomen. It surrounds the urinary bladder, the last portion of the large intestine, and, in women, the reproductive organs.

## • FACT FILE •

The spinal column joins the pelvis at the sacroiliac joints. The thighbones join the lower part of the pelvis with large ball-and-socket hip joints that allow the legs to move in many directions, as shown below.

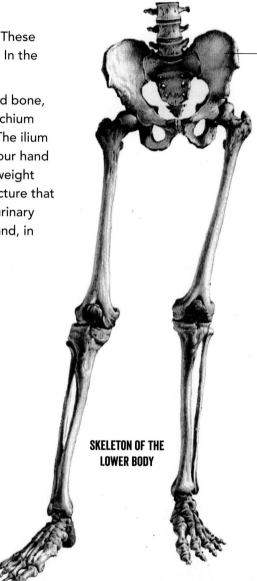

Pelvis

**SKELETON OF THE LOWER BODY**

A female's pelvis is flatter and broader than a male's and it has a larger central cavity.

# WHERE IS
# THE COCCYX SITUATED?

The coccyx is situated at the base of the spine. The axial skeleton is made up of the bones of the head, neck and trunk. The spine forms an axis that supports the other parts of the body. The skull is at the top of the spine. The spine consists of separate bones, called vertebrae, with fibrous discs between them. The ribs are attached to the thoracic vertebrae. There are usually 12 ribs on each side of the body; they protect the heart and lungs, and act as a bellows box for the breathing process.

The five lumbar vertebrae lie in the lower part of the back. Below the last lumbar vertebra is the sacrum, followed by the coccyx. In children, four separate bones make up the coccyx. The three lowest of these bones often fuse together during adulthood to form a beak-like bone. The point where the sacrum and coccyx meet remains fibrous throughout life.

**?** DID YOU KNOW THAT THE COCCYX IS ALSO KNOWN AS THE TAILBONE? THAT IS BECAUSE IT IS CONSIDERED TO BE A REMNANT OF THE TAIL OUR APE-LIKE ANCESTORS WOULD HAVE HAD.

Coccyx

**FACT FILE**

Muscles can't push, they can only pull. Muscles are pulling gently against each other most of the time. This keeps them firm and stops them from becoming floppy. Muscles are joined to bones by tough bands called tendons.

# WHERE IS THE SMALLEST BONE IN YOUR BODY?

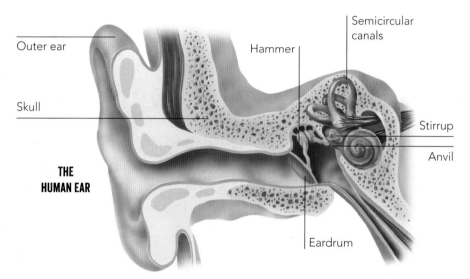

Outer ear

Skull

**THE HUMAN EAR**

Hammer

Semicircular canals

Stirrup

Anvil

Eardrum

The smallest bone in the body is called the stirrup. It is in the middle ear and is part of the system that carries sound signals to the brain. At only 3 mm (⅛ in) long, the stirrup is about the size of a grain of rice. The footplate of the stirrup bone is attached to a membrane called the oval window, which leads to the inner ear. It is connected to two other very small bones called the hammer and the anvil. All three of these bones are joined to the eardrum, where sound is collected before it is sent in the form of nerve signals to the brain.

The ear is a very important organ for keeping our sense of balance. Without a sense of balance, we could not hold our body steady, and we would stagger and fall when we tried to move.

**THE INNER EAR IS NO LARGER IN CIRCUMFERENCE THAN THE ERASER AT THE END OF YOUR PENCIL!**

**• FACT FILE •**

Some people suffer from motion sickness when they travel by boat, car or aeroplane. Motion sickness is caused by excessive stimulation of the components within the inner ear. But researchers do not know why some people develop motion sickness more easily than others.

# WHERE IS
# THE MANDIBLE?

Mandible

There are fourteen bones in the face; the two that make up the jaw are the maxillae (upper jaw) and the mandible (lower jaw). The mandible, like the maxilla, contains sockets for the 32 teeth, which are embedded in fibrous tissue. Teeth are hard, bonelike structures in the upper and lower jaws of human beings and many animals.

Muscles in the head are important to the processes of chewing and swallowing. They are responsible for facial expressions, such as smiling or frowning. A system of muscles and tendons connects the head to the spinal column, the collarbone and the shoulder blades. These muscles and tendons control the movement of the head.

## • FACT FILE •

The lower jaw is the only bony part of the face that moves. There are 32 permanent teeth, 16 in each jaw. Each jaw has four incisors, two canines, four premolars and six molars.

# WHY DO PEOPLE HAVE X-RAYS TAKEN?

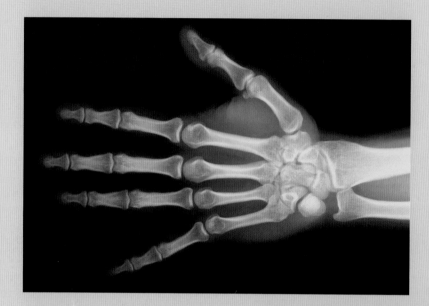

In German an X-ray is called *das Roentgen* and is named after William Roentgen, the scientist who discovered it.

If we have an accident, often we go to hospital to have an X-ray taken of our body to see if we have any broken bones. The X-ray 'picture' is a shadowgraph or shadow picture. X-rays pass through the part of the body being X-rayed and cast shadows on the film. The film is coated with a sensitive emulsion on both sides. After it is exposed, it is developed like ordinary photographic film.

X-rays do not pass through bones and other objects so they cast denser shadows which show up as light areas on the film. This will show the doctor whether any bone has been broken or dislocated.

## • FACT FILE •

Like X-rays, ultrasonic sound waves travel into the body and are bounced back by the organs inside. A screen can display the reflected sound as a picture. This is used to scan an unborn baby in a mother's womb.

# HOW DOES A BROKEN BONE HEAL?

Mending a broken bone is somewhat like mending a broken saucer, except the doctor doesn't have to apply any glue. This is produced by connective tissue cells of the bone itself. When bone is broken, bone and soft tissues around the break are torn and injured. Some of the injured tissue dies. The whole area containing the bone ends and the soft tissue is bound together by clotted blood and lymph.

Just a few hours after the break, young tissue cells begin to appear – the first step in repairing the fracture. These cells multiply quickly and become filled with calcium. Within 72 to 96 hours after the break, these cells form a tissue that unites the ends of the bones. More calcium is deposited in this newly formed tissue, which eventually helps form hard bone, developing into normal bone over a period of months.

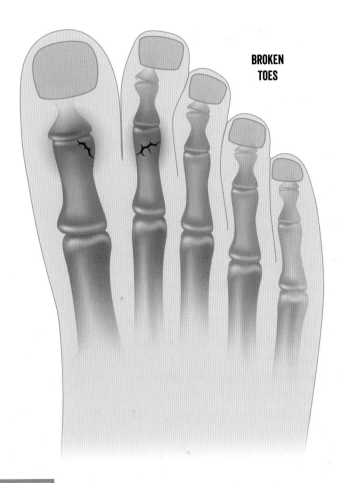

**BROKEN TOES**

## FACT FILE

A plaster cast is usually applied to a broken limb in order to keep the bone still and the broken edges in perfect alignment.

Bone tissue has an amazing ability to rebuild itself.

# HOW DO
# JOINTS WORK?

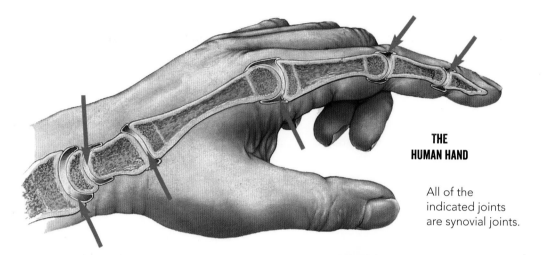

**THE HUMAN HAND**

All of the indicated joints are synovial joints.

The human body has more than 100 joints. Synovial joints – for example, the elbows, knuckles and wrists – are designed to allow a large range of movements and are lined with a slippery coating called synovial fluid. Some joints in the body only allow a small amount of movement between the bones, but if their effect is combined with lots of joints in close proximity, the result is greater flexibility. The bones in the wrist, ankle and spinal column all work like this. In the synovial joint the ends of the bones are held together by tough straps called ligaments. These bridge the gap between the bones and are anchored onto them at each end. Where bone ends move against each other, they are covered with cartilage, or gristle. This is shiny, smooth and slightly rubbery. It allows the bone ends to slide past each other with very little friction.

**DID YOU KNOW THAT THE ENDS OF MOST BONES ARE COVERED WITH TOUGH RUBBERY CARTILAGE, WHICH CUSHIONS THEM FROM IMPACT AS WE MOVE?**

## • FACT FILE •

Regular exercise improves muscle strength and endurance, and keeps the body supple. It can also improve your body shape and posture as well as strengthening your heart and improving your blood flow. Exercise will generally make you feel much better and help you to sleep more soundly.

# WHEN ARE
# DIFFERENT JOINTS REQUIRED?

A joint is the meeting point between bones and usually controls the amount of movement. Some joints have to be strong, while others need to be very mobile. As it is not possible for joints to be both strong and mobile we require many different kinds of joints:

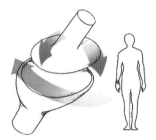

**PIVOT JOINT**
Allows rotation but no other movement.

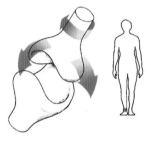

**BALL-AND-SOCKET JOINT**
A joint freely moving in all directions.

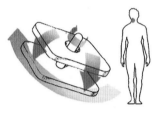

**SADDLE JOINT**
Allows movement in two directions, but without rotation.

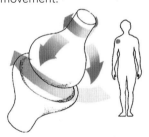

**HINGE JOINT**
Allows extension and flexion.

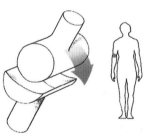

**CONDYLAR JOINT**
This is similar to a hinge joint, but with slight rotation to allow the joint to 'lock' into an extended position.

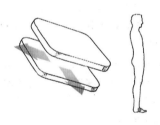

**ELLIPSOID JOINT**
Allows circular and bending movement but no rotation.

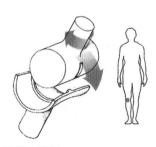

**PLANE JOINT**
A flat surface allows the bones to slide on each other, but they are restricted by ligaments.

## FACT FILE

The knee joint is the largest and most complex joint in the body. As it reaches full extension it rotates slightly and 'locks' into a rigid limb from hip to ankle.

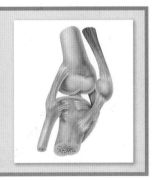

# WHERE IS THE LARGEST JOINT IN THE BODY?

The knee joint is the largest and most complex joint in the body.

The knee is the joint where the thighbone meets the large bone of the lower leg. The knee moves like a hinge, but it can also rotate and move a little from side to side.

The knee is more likely to be damaged than most other joints because it is subject to tremendous forces during vigorous activity. Most of the knee injuries that occur in football and other sports result from twisting the joint.

The knee ligaments are the strongest connections between the femur and the tibia. They prevent the bones moving out of position.

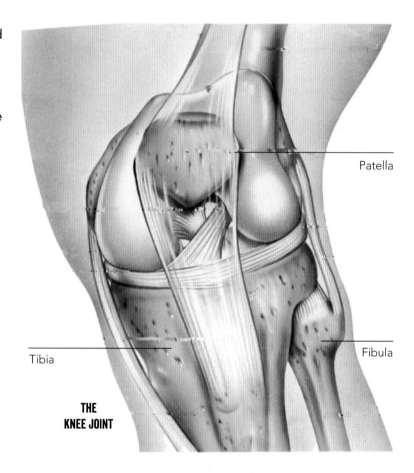

Patella

Tibia

Fibula

**THE KNEE JOINT**

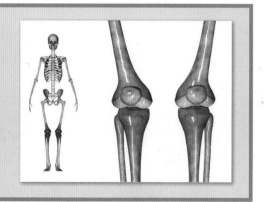

**THERE ARE AS MANY AS 30 JOINT SURFACES IN THE HUMAN WRIST AND HAND!**

# WHERE IS
# YOUR ACHILLES TENDON?

A tendon, also called a sinew, is a strong white cord that attaches muscles to bones and we have them all over our body. The Achilles tendon is the tendon at the back of the ankle. It attaches the muscles of the calf to the heel bone and is one of the strongest tendons in the body.

The Achilles tendon may rupture as the result of a powerful upward movement of the foot or a blow to the calf when the calf muscles are contracted. This injury most commonly occurs in people over the age of 30 who compete in sports that involve running. Complete rupture is often accompanied by a snap, severe pain and the inability to push off or stand on the toes. Ice should be applied to the back of the ankle, and the leg should be raised and immobilized. Surgery may be needed to sew the tendon together. The person should keep their weight off the injured leg for up to two months before progressing to gradual stretching and strengthening exercises. Full recovery may take a year or more.

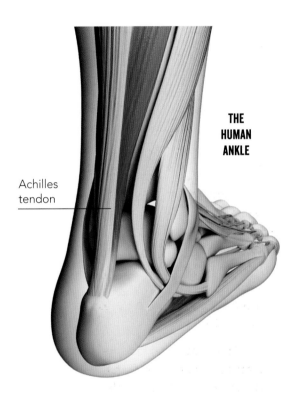

**THE HUMAN ANKLE**

Achilles tendon

**FACT FILE**

Thirty-five powerful muscles move the human hand. Fifteen are in the forearm rather than in the hand itself. This arrangement gives great strength to the hand without making the fingers so thick with muscles that they would be difficult to move.

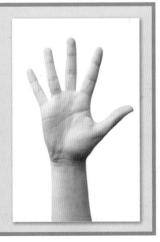

**?**

**DID YOU KNOW THAT THE NAME ACHILLES TENDON COMES FROM THE LEGEND OF ACHILLES, A GREEK HERO KILLED BY AN ARROW IN THE HEEL?**

# WHEN IS CONNECTIVE TISSUE NEEDED?

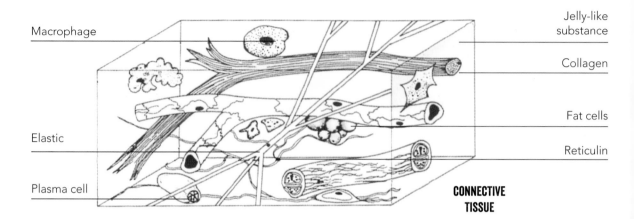

Macrophage

Jelly-like substance

Collagen

Fat cells

Elastic

Reticulin

Plasma cell

**CONNECTIVE TISSUE**

The skeleton is the framework of our bodies that keeps the organs, blood vessels and nerves in place and also acts as protection. The connective tissue is needed to act as a support and to bind them all together. It also supplies the ligaments and tendons for the joints and muscles, tethers the larger organs to keep them in place, and provides softness for protection and rigidity in the form of cartilage.

There are many forms of connective tissue, but they are all developed from the same jelly-like substance, which is made up of salts, water, protein and carbohydrate. There are other elements inside this jelly: elastic threads to give elasticity; collagen to give strength; reticulin to give support; white cells and macrophages to fight infection; fat cells for storage; and finally plasma cells to produce antibodies.

**• FACT FILE •**

The shape and appearance of a cell depends on what job it does. Cells consist of jelly-like cytoplasm, surrounded by a membrane. Nutrients pass through this membrane and substances produced by the cell leave in the same way.

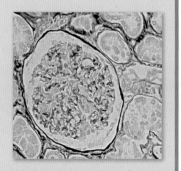

# WHAT DOES A TENDON SHEATH PROTECT?

The tendon sheath is a double-walled sleeve designed to isolate, protect and lubricate the tendon to reduce the possibility of damage from pressure or friction. The space between the two layers of the tendon sheath contains fluid so that these layers slide over each other easily.

A tendon, also called a sinew, is a strong white cord that attaches muscles to bones. Muscles move bones by pulling on tendons. Some tendons are round, others are long or flat. One end of a tendon rises from the end of a muscle; the other end is woven into the substance of a bone. The tendon may slide up and down inside a sheath of fibrous tissue, in the same way that an arm moves in a coat sleeve. Tendons at the ankle and wrist are enclosed in sheaths at the points where they cross or are in close contact with other structures.

**A tendon is a cordlike bundle of connective tissue.**

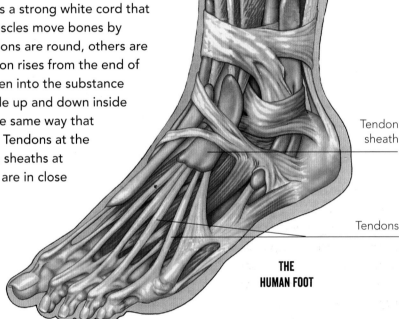

Tendon sheath

Tendons

**THE HUMAN FOOT**

**• FACT FILE •**

Most muscles can be controlled by consciously thinking about them – they move when you want them to. They are called voluntary muscles and there are more than 600 of them in your body. We use 200 voluntary muscles every time we take a step.

# HOW MANY MUSCLES ARE THERE IN THE HUMAN BODY?

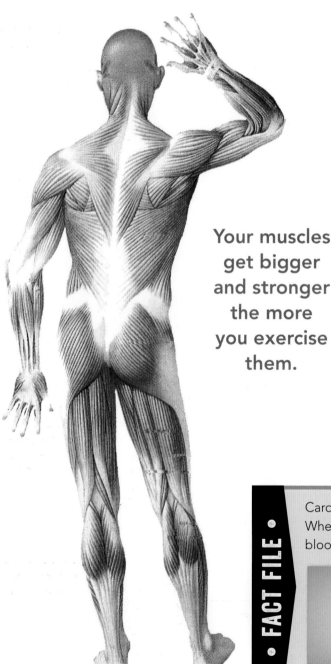

Your muscles get bigger and stronger the more you exercise them.

The human body has more than 600 major muscles. About 240 of them have specific names.

There are two main types of muscle: (1) skeletal muscle and (2) smooth muscle. A third kind of muscle, called cardiac muscle, has characteristics of both skeletal and smooth muscle. It is found only in the heart.

Skeletal muscles help hold the bones of the skeleton together and give the body shape. They also make the body move. Skeletal muscles make up a large part of the legs, arms, abdomen, chest, neck and face. These muscles vary greatly in size, depending on the type of jobs they do. For example, eye muscles are small and fairly weak, but the muscles of the thigh are large and strong.

## FACT FILE

Cardiac muscle makes up the walls of the heart. When cardiac muscle cells contract, they push blood out of the heart and into the arteries.

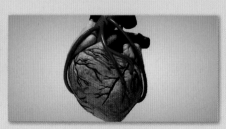

# HOW DO MUSCLES WORK?

There are 639 muscles in the human body, each comprising around ten million muscle cells. Each of these cells is like a motor containing ten cylinders arranged in a row. The cylinders are tiny boxes that contain fluid and when a muscle contracts the brain sends a message to these tiny boxes. For a fraction of a second, the fluid in the tiny box congeals; then it becomes fluid again. It is this action that causes the muscle to move.

When a muscle is stimulated into action, it reacts quickly – it may contract in less than one-tenth of a second. But before it has time to relax, another message comes along. It contracts again and again. All these contractions take place so quickly that they become fused into one action with the result that the muscle performs one smooth, continuous action.

## • FACT FILE •

When two muscles work against each other, they are always slightly contracted. This is called muscle tone. Active people tend to have better muscle tone.

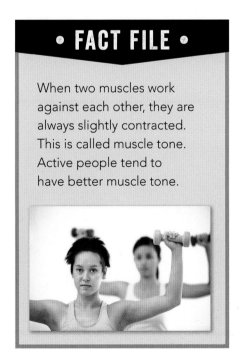

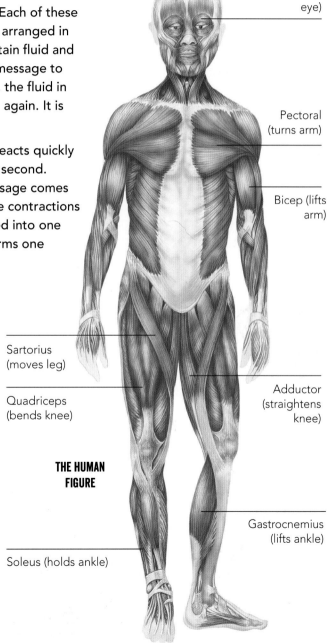

Orbicularis oculi (narrows eye)

Pectoral (turns arm)

Bicep (lifts arm)

Sartorius (moves leg)

Quadriceps (bends knee)

Adductor (straightens knee)

**THE HUMAN FIGURE**

Gastrocnemius (lifts ankle)

Soleus (holds ankle)

# HOW CAN
# MUSCLES WORK IN PAIRS?

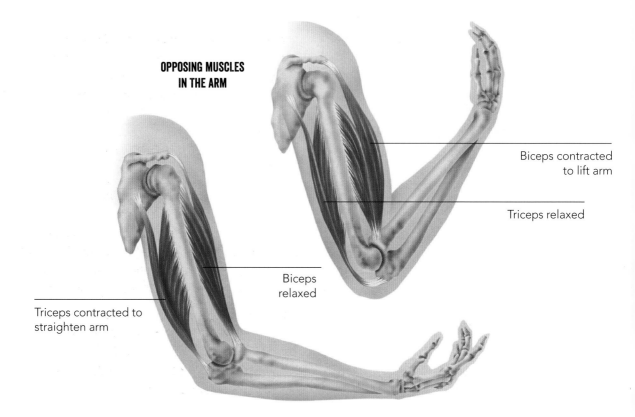

**OPPOSING MUSCLES IN THE ARM**

Biceps contracted to lift arm

Triceps relaxed

Biceps relaxed

Triceps contracted to straighten arm

Muscles actually work in pairs. A muscle can only pull in one direction so it needs another muscle to pull in the opposite direction in order to return a bone to its original position. When you lift your forearm, the biceps muscle shortens to lift the bone. When you straighten your arm, the triceps muscle pulls it back again and the biceps relaxes. The same action takes place in your legs when you walk and run, and when you move your fingers and toes.

**• FACT FILE •**

Our metabolism is the sum of all chemical activity in our cells that breaks down the food we take in. Our metabolic rate increases with vigorous exercise, which means that we use the energy produced by food much more efficiently.

# HOW DO MUSCLES RESPOND TO EXERCISE?

**While exercise is good for the body and muscles, rest is just as important.**

Muscles are made up of long, thin cells called muscle fibres. But muscles differ in what they do and how they do it. When a muscle contracts, it produces an acid known as lactic acid. This acid is like a poison, with the effect of making you feel tired, by making the muscles feel tired. If the lactic acid is removed from a tired muscle, it stops feeling tired and you can go right to work again!

But, of course, lactic acid is not removed normally when you exercise and various toxins are produced when muscles are active. They are carried by the blood through the body and cause tiredness throughout the entire body, especially in the brain. So feeling tired after exercise is really the result of a kind of internal poisoning.

However, the body needs this feeling of tiredness so that it will want to rest. During rest, waste products are removed, the cells recuperate, nerve cells of the brain recharge the batteries and the joints replace their supplies of lubricant they have used up.

## • FACT FILE •

The knee is a typical load-bearing joint. The ends of the bone are cushioned by a pad of cartilage to protect them from impact. Wear and tear is minimized by a lubricant called synovial fluid.

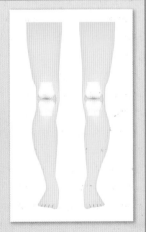

# WHERE ARE THE SMOOTH MUSCLES FOUND?

Smooth muscles are found in the walls of the stomach, intestines, blood vessels and bladder. They operate slowly and automatically in a natural, rhythmic pattern of contraction followed by relaxation. In this way, they control various body processes. For example, the steady action of smooth muscles in the stomach and intestines moves food along for digestion. Because they are not under conscious control by the brain, smooth muscles are also known as involuntary muscles. Smooth muscles are stimulated by a special set of nerves that belong to the autonomic nervous system, and by body chemicals.

## There are three types of muscle in the body: cardiac, smooth and skeletal.

### • FACT FILE •

Muscle cells are excitable because the membrane of each cell is electrically charged. Thus, a muscle cell is said to have electric potential.

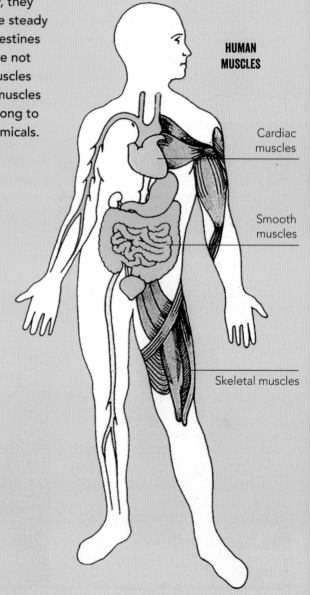

HUMAN
MUSCLES

Cardiac muscles

Smooth muscles

Skeletal muscles

# WHICH IS THE LARGEST MUSCLE IN YOUR BODY?

The largest muscle in the human body is called the gluteus maximus and it is one of three muscles situated in the buttocks. The other two are the gluteus medius and the gluteus minimus. Collectively, the three are known as the gluteal muscles (sometimes referred to as the 'glutes'). The gluteus maximus has much to do with supporting the torso to keep the body erect – hence its size and strength.

The smallest muscle in the body is the stapedius, which can be found in the middle ear. A muscle is the tough, elastic tissue that makes body parts move. Muscles are found throughout the body. As a person grows, the muscles also get bigger. People use muscles to make various movements.

## • FACT FILE •

Among the most powerful muscles are the masseters, one on each side of the face. The longest muscle is the sartorius, which runs from the side of the waist, diagonally down across the front of the thigh to the inside of the knee.

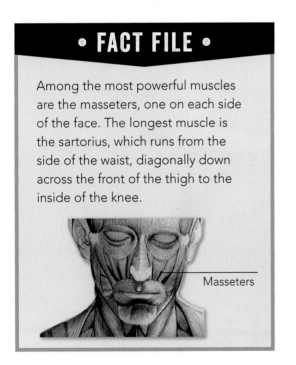

Masseters

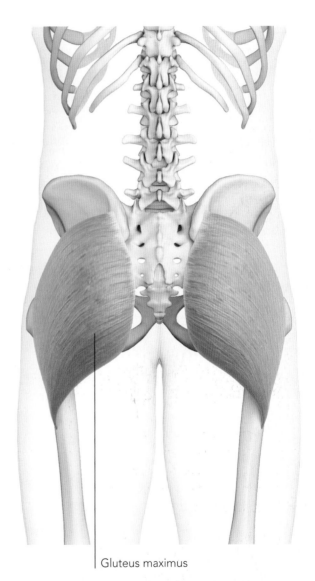

Gluteus maximus

**AT JUST OVER 1MM LONG, THE STAPEDIUS IS THE SMALLEST SKELETAL MUSCLE IN THE BODY! IT IS FOUND IN THE EAR.**

# CIRCULATION
# AND RESPIRATION

# CONTENTS

# WHAT IS OUR CIRCULATORY SYSTEM?

The circulatory system is a network that carries blood throughout the body. The human circulatory system supplies the cells of the body with the food and oxygen they need to survive. At the same time, it carries carbon dioxide and other wastes away from the cells. The circulatory system also helps regulate the temperature of the body and carries substances that protect the body from disease. In addition, the system transports chemical substances called hormones, which help regulate the activities of various parts of the body. The blood vessels form a complicated system of connecting tubes throughout the body. There are three major types of these blood vessels. Arteries carry blood from the heart. Veins return blood to the heart. Capillaries are extremely tiny vessels that connect the arteries and the veins.

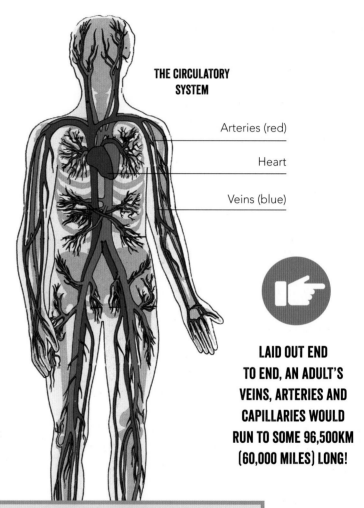

**THE CIRCULATORY SYSTEM**

Arteries (red)

Heart

Veins (blue)

**LAID OUT END TO END, AN ADULT'S VEINS, ARTERIES AND CAPILLARIES WOULD RUN TO SOME 96,500KM (60,000 MILES) LONG!**

## FACT FILE

The human circulatory system has three main parts: the heart, the blood vessels and the blood. A watery fluid called lymph, and the vessels that carry it, are sometimes considered a part of the circulatory system.

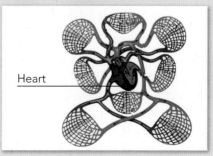

Heart

# WHAT IS CORONARY CIRCULATION?

Coronary circulation is part of the systemic circulatory system that supplies blood to, and provides drainage from, the tissues of the heart. In the human heart, two coronary arteries arise from the aorta just beyond the semilunar valves; during diastole (when the heart's chambers dilute and fill with blood) the increased aortic pressure above the valves forces blood into the coronary arteries and then into the musculature of the heart. Deoxygenated blood is returned to the chambers of the heart via coronary veins and then drained into the right ventricle below the tricuspid valve.

The heart normally extracts 70 to 75 per cent of the available oxygen from the blood in coronary circulation, which is much more than the amount extracted by other organs from their circulations. Obstruction of a coronary artery, depriving the heart tissue of oxygen-rich blood, leads to death of part of the heart muscle in severe cases.

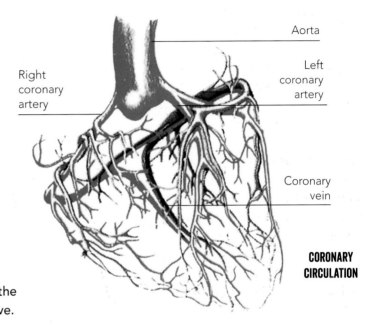

Aorta

Left coronary artery

Right coronary artery

Coronary vein

**CORONARY CIRCULATION**

An adult has an average resting heart rate of about 75 beats per minute.

## FACT FILE

Sometimes the heart valves become stiff or leaky. They can be replaced during surgery, using valves made from tissue taken from an animal, or by artificial valves made of metal and plastic.

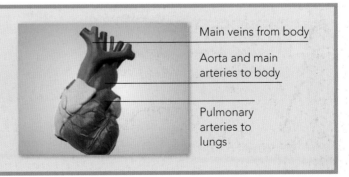

Main veins from body

Aorta and main arteries to body

Pulmonary arteries to lungs

# HOW DOES OUR BLOOD CIRCULATE?

Blood is pumped in a continuous flow from the heart. Blood flows inside a network of tubes called blood vessels – arteries, veins and capillaries.

The blood in arteries comes straight from the heart and is pumped under pressure, so the artery walls are thick and muscular. Blood moves from arteries to veins through tiny capillaries, which are about one-tenth the thickness of a human hair. Capillaries are so narrow that red blood cells have to squash themselves up to pass through. Veins return blood to the heart, and because the pressure is lower, they have thinner walls than arteries.

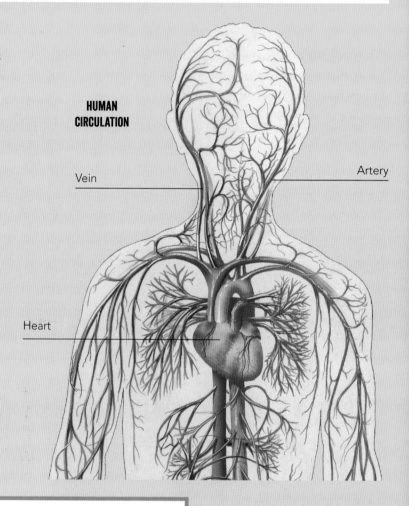

**HUMAN CIRCULATION**

Vein

Artery

Heart

**FACT FILE**

The heart beats about 100,000 times a day – that's more than 36 million times a year! The heart can pump 7 litres (14 pints) of blood around your body in just one minute; this heart rate can be increased by exercise.

**IT'S A FACT THAT A WOMAN'S HEART BEATS FASTER THAN A MAN'S!**

# HOW DOES THE HEART WORK?

The heart is a fist-sized muscular organ that pumps blood around the body. It is actually two pumps that are joined together.

At the top of each side of the heart is a thin-walled chamber called the atrium, which receives blood that returns to the heart through the veins. Once the atrium is filled, it contracts and squeezes its blood into a much more muscular chamber called the ventricle. The ventricle contracts in turn and forces blood at high pressure along the arteries and off to the lungs or the rest of the body.

A system of oneway valves stops the blood from leaking back into the heart. The left side of the heart pumps blood to the lungs to collect more oxygen.

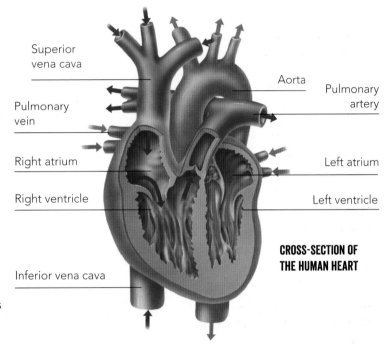

Superior vena cava

Aorta

Pulmonary artery

Pulmonary vein

Right atrium

Left atrium

Right ventricle

Left ventricle

Inferior vena cava

**CROSS-SECTION OF THE HUMAN HEART**

**DID YOU KNOW THAT THE ANCIENT EGYPTIANS WERE AMONG THE FIRST TO BELIEVE THAT THE HEART (AND NOT THE BRAIN) WAS THE CENTRE OF EMOTION, MEMORY AND WISDOM?**

## • FACT FILE •

An electrocardiogram, or ECG, measures the electrical signals that the heart produces as it beats. These signals change when a person suffers from certain medical conditions that affect the heart. They are measured by attaching wires to the chest near the heart. A doctor can study results as printed information.

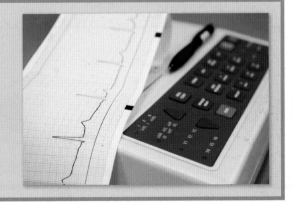

# WHEN DO PEOPLE GET HEART ATTACKS?

Your heart is a powerful muscle that pumps blood around your body. It is only the size of your fist and weighs less than ½kg (1lb). It pumps 18,000 litres (31,756pt) of blood around your body a day.

A heart attack can occur when either or both sides of the heart fail to pump sufficient blood to meet the needs of our body. Other prominent causes of a heart attack are abnormally high blood pressure (hypertension), accumulation of fatty deposits in the coronary arteries (atheroma), the presence of a blod clot in the coronary arteries (coronary atherosclerosis), and rheumatic heart disease.

A person with left-sided heart failure experiences shortness of breath after exertion, difficulty in breathing while lying down, spasms of breathlessness at night and abnormally high pressure in the pulmonary veins. A person with right-sided failure experiences abnormally high pressure in the systemic veins, enlargement of the liver, and accumulation of fluid in the legs. A person with failure of both ventricles has an enlarged heart that beats in gallop rhythm – that is, in groups of three sounds rather than two.

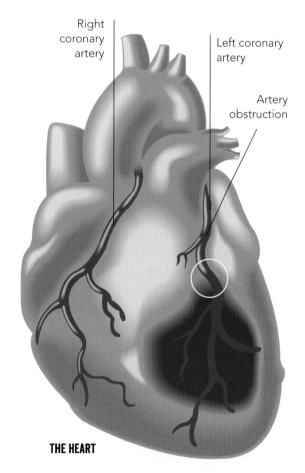

Right coronary artery

Left coronary artery

Artery obstruction

**THE HEART**

## FACT FILE

The muscle that makes up the walls of the heart, called cardiac muscle or myocardium, never ceases working and needs a continuing supply of blood.

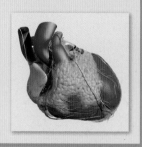

Run upstairs quickly, and you will soon feel your heart thumping away inside your rib cage.

# WHEN DOES THE HEART STOP BEATING?

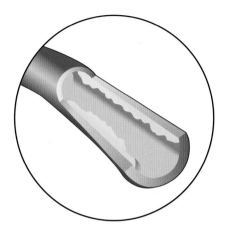

Atheroma

Your heart is a muscular pump that never stops beating. It has its own timing device that produces tiny electrical signals. These signals cause the heart muscle to contract rhythmically. The pump on the right side of the heart receives blood that has been pumped around the body. This blood is dark red and has used up most of its oxygen. The right pump sends it on a short circuit through the lungs that surround the heart. The blood comes back bright red and rich in oxygen, to the heart's left side, ready for its journey around the body. When the heart stops beating, body tissues no longer receive fresh blood carrying oxygen and nutrients. So life ends.

However, in a hospital, the cardiopulmonary machine can take over the job of heart and lungs. This means doctors can resuscitate people or carry out operations on the heart, such as replacing diseased valves.

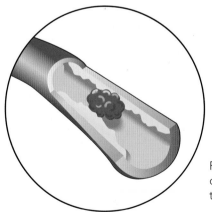

Formation of a clot that clogs the artery

## • FACT FILE •

When the body is very active, the heart can pump 90 litres (20 gallons) of blood each minute. That would fill a bathtub within two minutes.

**DID YOU KNOW THAT THE BLOOD IN YOUR VEINS APPEARS BLUE OWING TO A TRICK OF THE LIGHT? IN REALITY, THIS BLOOD IS A VERY DARK RED.**

# WHY ARE ARTERIES DIFFERENT FROM VEINS?

Arteries and veins are different from one another because they have different parts to play in our blood's circulation. Arteries take blood from the heart to the rest of the body, while veins return it. Blood is pumped from the right side of the heart through the pulmonary artery to the lungs and returns through the pulmonary vein to the left side of the heart. From there it is pumped via the large artery called the aorta to the rest of the body and eventually returns to the right side of the heart again through the veins known as the inferior vena cava, from the legs and abdomen, and superior vena cava, from the head, neck and arms.

Blood is forced through the arteries in spurts at high pressure, so their walls are thick and flexible and expand with every pulse of blood. In the veins, blood pressure is low and the blood flow is steadier. The walls of veins are thin and collapsible and valves prevent the blood flowing back in the wrong direction.

Smooth muscle

Protective fibrous covering

Connective tissue

Smooth layer of cells

**THE BLOOD VESSELS**

Artery          Vein

In general, arteries lie deep within the body, and veins nearer the surface. So the blood vessels you can see on your hands are veins.

## FACT FILE

Blood contains red and white blood cells that float inside a liquid called plasma. It also contains thousands of different substances needed by the body. Blood carries all these things round the body and also removes waste products.

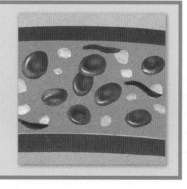

# WHAT MAKES
# THE HEARTBEAT SOUND?

Aorta and main arteries to body

Pulmonary artery

Main veins (vena cavae) from body

**1.** **2.** **3.** **4.**

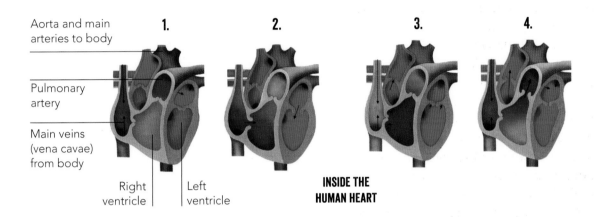

Right ventricle | Left ventricle

**INSIDE THE HUMAN HEART**

Both sides of the heart pump blood at the same time. As the right ventricle contracts and sends blood to the lungs, the left ventricle also contracts and squeezes blood out to the body. The heart's cycle of activity has two stages, systole and diastole. Systole occurs when the ventricles contract. Diastole is the stage when the ventricles relax and the atria contract.

One complete cycle of contraction and relaxation – called a cardiac cycle – makes up one heartbeat. During each cardiac cycle, the heart valves open and close. Closing of the valves produces most of the 'lub dub' sound of a heartbeat, which doctors can hear with an instrument called a stethoscope. As the ventricles contract, the mitral and tricuspid valves close, causing the first sound (1). Immediately after the valves close, pressure in the ventricles forces the aortic and pulmonic valves to open (2). After a contraction ends, pressure in the ventricles drops (3). The aortic and pulmonic valves then close, causing most of the second heart sound (4).

## • FACT FILE •

The heart of an average person at rest beats 60 to 80 times each minute. Each beat sends about 70ml (2½oz) of blood out of each ventricle. This means that, at rest, the heart pumps some 11 litres (20pt) of blood each minute.

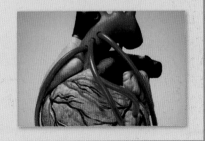

# WHY DOESN'T BLOOD FLOW BACKWARDS?

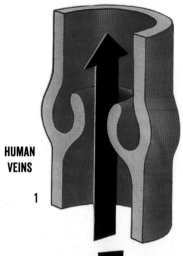

**HUMAN VEINS**

1

2

A vein is a blood vessel that carries blood towards the heart. The blood circulates in the body through a system of tubes called blood vessels. The blood in your veins travels quite slowly, and many large veins have valves to stop the blood from draining backwards towards the legs and feet.

Blood flowing forwards forces the valve flaps to open (1). Blood flowing back forces them to shut (2). The valves in the heart work in exactly the same way.

Blood is also helped along by the arm and leg muscles contracting. That is why, if you stand still for a long period of time, blood can collect in your legs and make them puffy and sore.

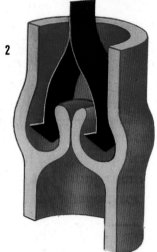

If you make a fist with your hand, that will give you a good idea as to the size of your heart.

## • FACT FILE •

The lymphatic system is one of the body's defences against infection. Harmful particles and bacteria that have entered the body are filtered out by small masses of tissue that lie along the lymphatic vessels. These bean-shaped masses are called lymph nodes.

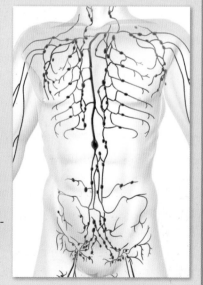

# WHERE ARE
# THE JUGULAR VEINS SITUATED?

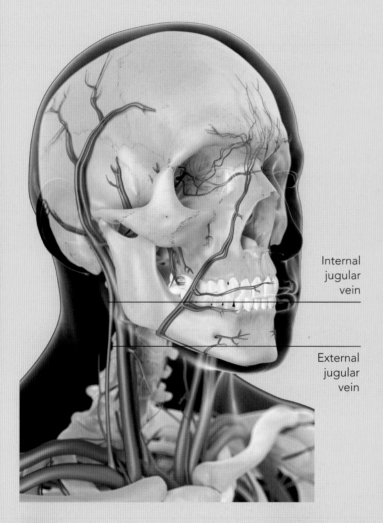

Internal jugular vein

External jugular vein

The jugular vein is the name of each of four large veins that return blood to the heart from the head and neck. The veins get their name from the Latin word *jugulus*, which means collarbone. There are two jugular veins on each side of the neck, known as the external and internal jugulars. The external jugulars lie close to the surface and carry blood from the outer parts of the head and neck to the heart. The internal jugulars lie further in and carry blood from the deeper tissues of the neck and from the interior of the skull. The internal jugular veins are much larger than the external, and are the ones commonly referred to as jugulars. Opening an internal jugular vein usually proves fatal, because of the rapid loss of blood.

**FACT FILE**

The whole of the autonomic system is controlled by an area of the brain called the hypothalamus. This receives information about any variations in your body.

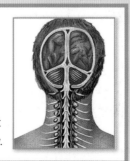

**?**

HAVE YOU EVER HEARD SOMEONE TALK ABOUT 'GOING FOR THE JUGULAR'? IT MEANS ATTACKING SOMEONE AT THEIR WEAKEST POINT, AND REFERS TO THE VULNERABILITY OF THE VEIN IF CUT.

# WHICH CELLS CARRY BLOOD AROUND THE BODY?

Platelets

Small and large lymphocytes

Monocyte

**BLOOD COMPONENTS**

Red blood cells

Red blood cells carry oxygen around the body. They are among the most numerous cells in the body, and some of the smallest. Each red cell is shaped like a doughnut without the hole poked completely through and its colour is due to the substance haemoglobin. Haemoglobin joins or attaches to oxygen and carries it around the body. Each red cell contains 250 million tiny particles, or molecules, of haemoglobin. Red blood cells live for three or four months, then they die and are broken apart. This means about three million red blood cells die every second – and the same number of new ones are made. Red blood cells, like white blood cells and platelets, are made in the jelly-like marrow inside bones.

**OUR BLOOD CONTAINS MILLIONS AND MILLIONS OF RED BLOOD CELLS – AROUND 25,000 BILLION IN AN AVERAGE PERSON.**

## FACT FILE

Blood is mostly made up of plasma and red blood cells. White blood cells and platelets make up a tiny proportion of the total. Plasma contains many dissolved substances such as blood sugar (glucose), hormones, body salts and minerals, unwanted wastes such as urea, disease-fighting antibodies, and dozens of others. Red and white blood corpuscles and platelets are suspended in the plasma.

Plasma

White blood cells

Red blood cells

# WHICH BLOOD GROUP ARE YOU?

**RECEPTOR**

|  | A | B | AB | O |
|---|---|---|---|---|

**DONOR**

| A | | | | |
| B | | | | |
| AB | | | | |
| O | | | | |

 COMPATIBLE

NON-COMPATIBLE

It is important to know what blood group someone is if they are about to become a donor. This is because certain kinds or groups of blood, when mixed together, may form clumps or clots, and this can be dangerous during a blood transfusion, when blood is given or donated by one person, to be put into another person, the recipient. Humans have four different blood groups, which were discovered in 1900, which can be tested using a system called ABO. A person can be either A, B, AB or O. A person with group O is a 'universal donor' whose blood can be given to almost anyone. A person with group AB is a 'universal recipient' who can receive blood from almost anyone.

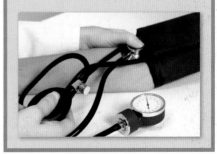

# HOW DO CUTS AND GRAZES HEAL THEMSELVES?

When we cut or graze ourselves, the body is able to heal itself. When the skin incurs a wound, platelets in the blood congregate at the site of the wound to form a temporary clot. This usually happens as soon as a wound is exposed to the air. This quickly plugs the wound. White blood cells gather around the wound site to kill invading microbes, helping to prevent infection.

New cells eventually grow into the wound replacing the damaged tissue. For a small cut or graze, this usually takes a couple of days. Soon the clotted material, which has formed a scab, falls off to reveal clean, new skin underneath. Sometimes we protect our grazes and cuts with plasters whilst our bodies deal with the repair.

**STAGES OF BLOOD CLOTTING**

Tissue factor

Fibrinogen

1

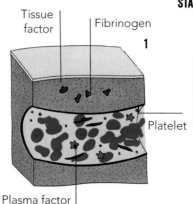

Platelet

2

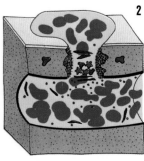

Plasma factor

3

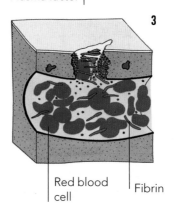

4

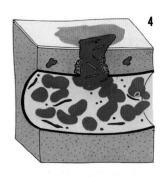

Red blood cell

Fibrin

## FACT FILE

Cells need food, oxygen and water in order to survive. Food and water are supplied by the blood and other body fluids, which also carry away wastes. Blood also contains food substances and chemicals needed by the cell.

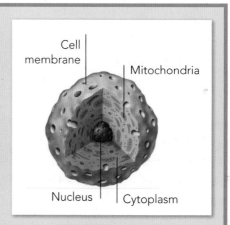

Cell membrane

Mitochondria

Nucleus

Cytoplasm

**?**

**DID YOU KNOW THAT YOUR BLOOD MAKES UP ABOUT EIGHT PER CENT OF YOUR BODY WEIGHT?**

# WHAT IS HAEMOPHILIA?

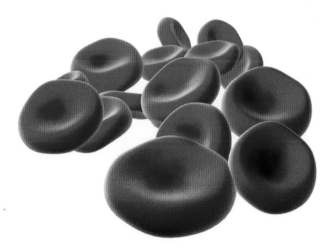

Red blood cells

Haemophilia is an inherited deficiency in which the substance necessary for blood clotting, called Factor 8, is missing. This is a painful condition because haemophiliacs can have swollen joints where the blood leaks into them. More seriously, even a slight cut or bump can be dangerous if the bleeding cannot be stopped. The transmission of this condition is linked to gender, being present mostly in males but carried solely by females. Sons of a haemophiliac male will not inheret the deficiency. Daughters, although they show no outward symptoms themselves, may transmit this deficiency to their sons.

The condition can be treated by giving the haemophiliac doses of Factor 8 that has either been extracted from donated blood or has been synthesized in a laboratory.

## • FACT FILE •

When we look at other human bodies, we usually concentrate on the face. Our features are largely inherited, under control of the genes, which is why we resemble our parents.

## ?

DID YOU KNOW THAT QUEEN VICTORIA WAS A CARRIER OF HAEMOPHILIA? OF HER NINE CHILDREN, TWO DAUGHTERS CARRIED THE GENE AND ONE SON WAS AFFLICTED WITH THE DEFICIENCY.

# WHEN DOES THE SPLEEN PRODUCE RED BLOOD CELLS?

The spleen is one of the main filters of the blood. Not only do the reticular cells remove the old and worn-out blood cells, but they will also remove any abnormal cells. This applies in particular to red blood cells, but white cells and platelets are also filtered selectively by the spleen when it is necessary.

The spleen will also remove abnormal particles that are floating in the bloodstream. It therefore plays a very important part in ridding the body of harmful bacteria.

In some circumstances the spleen has a major role in the manufacture of new red blood cells. This does not happen in a healthy adult, but in people who have a bone marrow disease. The spleen and liver are major sites of red blood cell production. Another function of the spleen is to manufacture a great deal of the blood of a foetus while it is in the uterus during its period of gestation.

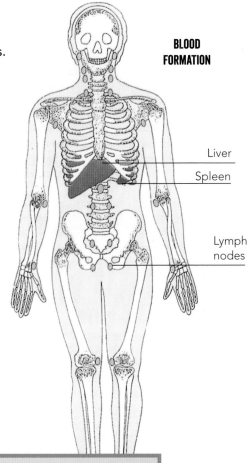

**BLOOD FORMATION**

Liver

Spleen

Lymph nodes

**A RED BLOOD CELL CAN MAKE A FULL CIRCUIT OF THE HUMAN BODY IN JUST 30 SECONDS!**

## • FACT FILE •

The spleen is situated in the top left-hand corner of the abdomen, just below the diaphragm. It lies in a relatively exposed position, which is why it is frequently damaged in accidents and has to be removed.

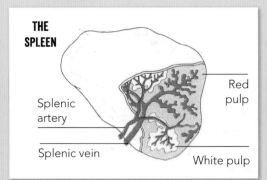

**THE SPLEEN**

Splenic artery

Splenic vein

Red pulp

White pulp

# WHEN DO RED AND WHITE BLOOD CELLS DIE?

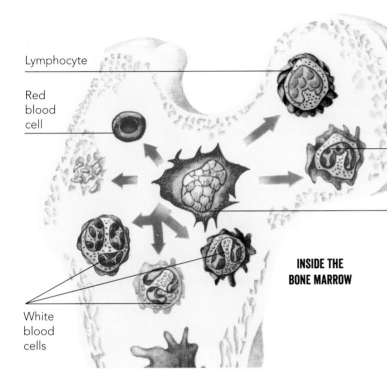

Lymphocyte

Red blood cell

Monocyte

Stem cell

White blood cells

**INSIDE THE BONE MARROW**

## • FACT FILE •

An adult body has about 5 litres (8½pt) of blood. At any one time, about 1,250ml (2pt) are in the arteries, 3,500ml (6pt) in the veins and 250ml (½pt) in the capillaries. The cells in blood flow through a capillary for only half a second before they move into the next type of vessels, small veins.

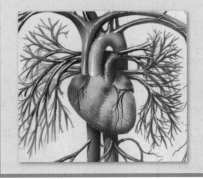

Both white and red blood cells are formed in the bone marrow. Each red blood cell measures about 7.5 microns (thousandths of a millimetre) in diameter and are shaped a little like doughnuts. They contain haemoglobin, which gives them their red pigment. There are five to six million red cells per cubic millimetre of blood. The red blood cell only survives about 120 days and the damaged and old cells are removed by the spleen and the liver.

A white blood cell can change shape, push out folds and finger-like projections and move along by oozing and crawling like an amoeba in a pond. These cells survive less than a week.

# HOW DO WE BREATHE?

Respiration, or breathing, is when you draw air in through the nose and mouth and into the lungs. Like all movements in the body, those of respiration rely on muscle power. There are two main sets of breathing muscles: the intercostal muscle and the diaphragm. Breathe in deeply and watch your ribs rise and your chest expand. Together these muscles make the chest bigger and stretch the spongy lungs inside. As the lungs enlarge, they suck in air down the windpipe. This is how we breathe in. Then the muscles relax. The ribs fall back down and the diaphragm resumes its domed shape as the spongy, elastic lungs spring back to their smaller size. The lungs blow some of their air up the windpipe. This is how we breathe out.

The movements of breathing are controlled by the brain. It sends out signals to make the muscles contract. The signals pass along nerves to the intercostal and diaphragm muscles, making them contract. This happens every few seconds throughout our life, even when you are asleep.

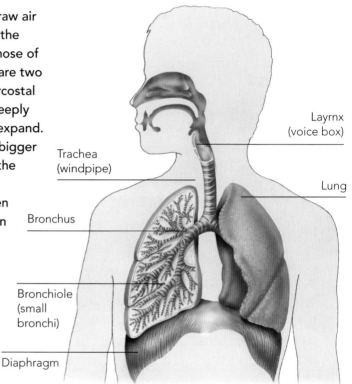

Layrnx (voice box)

Trachea (windpipe)

Lung

Bronchus

Bronchiole (small bronchi)

Diaphragm

**THE HUMAN RESPIRATORY SYSTEM**

**THERE ARE LITTLE HAIRS IN THE NOSE THAT CLEAN THE AIR WE INHALE, AS WELL AS WARMING IT BEFORE IT ENTERS THE BODY!**

**FACT FILE**

The average person at rest breathes in and out about 10–14 times per minute. If you sing or play instruments like trumpets, you need lots of puff. Learn to use the muscle under your lungs to get more lung power.

# WHERE DOES THE EXCHANGE OF GASES TAKE PLACE?

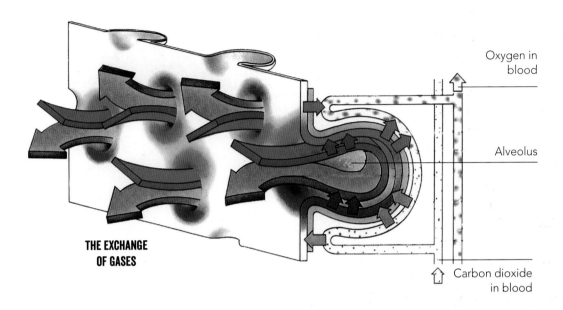

**THE EXCHANGE OF GASES**

Oxygen in blood

Alveolus

Carbon dioxide in blood

The exchange of gases takes place within the respiratory system. The primary function of the respiratory system is to supply the blood with oxygen in order for the blood to deliver oxygen to all parts of the body. The respiratory system does this through breathing. When we breathe, we inhale oxygen and exhale carbon dioxide. This is known as the exchange of gases, and is the body's means of getting oxygen to the blood. Oxygen enters the respiratory system through the mouth and the nose. It is the job of the diaphragm to help pump the carbon dioxide out of the lungs and pull the oxygen into the lungs. The diaphragm is a sheet of muscles that lies across the bottom of the chest cavity.

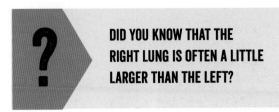

**?** DID YOU KNOW THAT THE RIGHT LUNG IS OFTEN A LITTLE LARGER THAN THE LEFT?

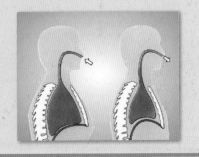

# WHAT IS INSIDE THE LUNGS?

You have two lungs, one in each side of your chest, enclosed by an airtight box.

The somewhat bullet-shaped lungs are suspended within the rib cage. They extend from just above the first rib down to the diaphragm, a muscular sheet that separates the chest cavity from the abdomen. A thin, tough membrane called the visceral pleura covers the outer surface of the lungs. The heart, large blood vessels and oesophagus (the tube connecting the mouth and stomach) lie between the two lungs.

Inside the lungs are tiny air sacs called alveoli, surrounded by capillaries. The walls of the alveoli and capillaries are so thin that oxygen and carbon dioxide can pass through them. The alveoli of an adult have a total surface area of 70m$^2$ (750ft$^2$) and the whole breathing apparatus is designed to bring fresh air as close as possible to the blood. Your lungs fill with air when you breathe in, and empty when you breathe out.

They go up and down rather like balloons, but they aren't just hollow bags. They are spongy organs made up of tightly packed tissue, nerves and blood vessels.

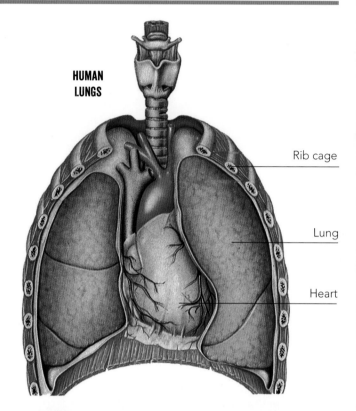

**HUMAN LUNGS**

Rib cage

Lung

Heart

**IF THE WALLS OF THE ALVEOLI COULD BE SPREAD OUT FLAT, THEY WOULD COVER ABOUT HALF A TENNIS COURT!**

## • FACT FILE •

Each alveolar duct in the lungs supplies about 20 alveoli. The very thin walls of each alveolus contain networks of extremely small blood vessels called pulmonary capillaries. Gas is exchanged between the blood in these capillaries and the gas in the alveoli.

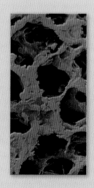

# WHEN DO WE COUGH?

**THE FASTEST SNEEZE ON RECORD BLASTED OUT AT AN AMAZING 166KM (103 MILES) PER HOUR!**

Coughing is the way in which the lungs dislodge anything that blocks the air passages. Usually these are only minor blockages caused by a build-up of mucus when you have a cold or chest infection. When you cough, your vocal cords press together to seal off the air passages. At the same time your chest muscles become tense, raising the pressure in your lungs. When you release the air it rushes out, carrying the obstruction with it.

The delicate alveoli inside the lungs can be damaged by many different things, thus causing us to cough. One is tobacco smoke, which clogs the alveoli and airways with thick tar. Others are the polluting gases that hover in the air of many big cities, coming from vehicle exhausts as well as factory and power-plant chimneys. Some types of industrial dust and particles floating in the air, such as asbestos or coal-mine dust can cause considerable damage to the lungs.

# WHAT IS BRONCHITIS?

Bronchitis is an inflammation of all or part of the bronchial tree (the bronchi), through which air passes into the lungs.

During the passage through the bronchi, microorganisms and other foreign bodies are removed from the air by tiny hairlike structures called cilia, which project from the cells that line the bronchial wall. These cilia have a wavelike motion and sweep the foreign material upward towards the trachea and larynx. Because of this irritation a thick mucus is produced by glands in the bronchial wall, which aids in the elimination of the foreign material. Such material and the secreted mucus stimulate nerve endings in the bronchial wall and cause you to cough in an effort to expel the foreign material.

Acute bronchitis is caused by any of a great number of agents and not a specific disease. It is most frequently caused by viruses responsible for upper respiratory infections and is, therefore, often part of the common cold.

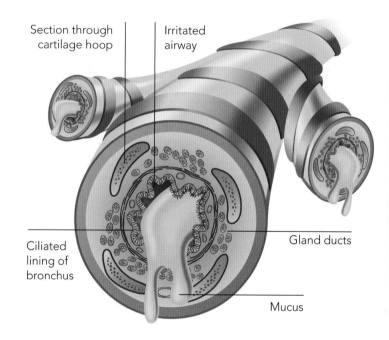

Section through cartilage hoop

Irritated airway

Ciliated lining of bronchus

Gland ducts

Mucus

**BRONCHITIS**

# WHERE WOULD
# YOU USE A BRONCHOSCOPE?

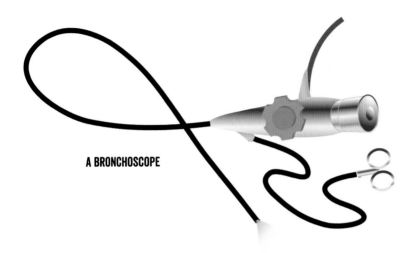

**A BRONCHOSCOPE**

In very polluted enivronments, wearing a facemask can reduce the inhalation of potentially harmful particles.

A bronchoscope would be used to examine the trachea and the bronchial tubes of the lungs. It is an instrument consisting of a hollow tube with a system of lights and mirrors.

A bronchoscope is inserted through the patient's mouth or nose into the throat and lungs. It enables a physician to detect diseased areas that cannot be seen by X-rays. Attachments, such as a sucking needle, forceps and brush can be added to a bronchoscope. Physicians use them to remove small tumours, pus, foreign bodies and samples of lung tissue.

## • FACT FILE •

Because the lungs must inhale the air from the environment, they are exposed to bacteria, viruses, dust and pollutants that are mixed with the air. A sticky fluid called mucus lines the airways and traps most of these foreign substances.

# DIGESTION
# AND EXCRETION

# CONTENTS

# HOW DO WE DIGEST FOOD?

Digestion is the process of changing the food we eat so that it can be used by the body.

In the mouth, the saliva helps break down starches. When food has been moistened and crushed in the mouth, it travels to the stomach. Here, the juices from the stomach wall are mixed with the food, helping to break down proteins into simpler forms to aid digestion. The starches continue to break down until the material in the stomach becomes too acid. The contents in the stomach are churned about to mix digestive juices throughout the food.

When the food becomes liquified it enters the small intestine. In the first part of the small intestine, the duodenum, digestion continues. Juices from the pancreas and liver help to further break down the foods. The breakdown of proteins is finished here, fats are split into finer parts, and starch digestion is completed. It is also in the small intestine that digested food is absorbed into the blood and lymph. Finally, in the large intestine, water is absorbed and the contents become more solid, so they can leave the body as waste material.

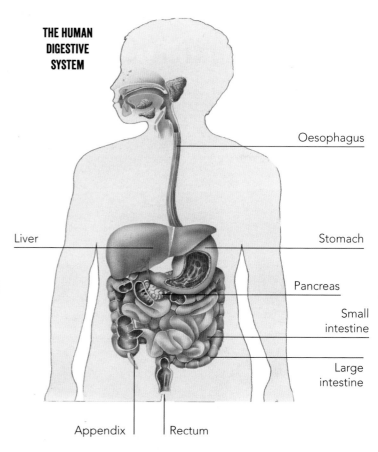

**THE HUMAN DIGESTIVE SYSTEM**

Oesophagus

Liver

Stomach

Pancreas

Small intestine

Large intestine

Appendix

Rectum

## FACT FILE

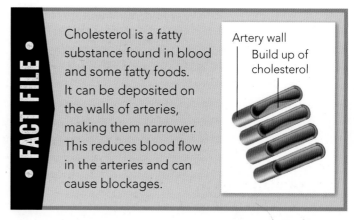

Cholesterol is a fatty substance found in blood and some fatty foods. It can be deposited on the walls of arteries, making them narrower. This reduces blood flow in the arteries and can cause blockages.

Artery wall

Build up of cholesterol

# WHERE DOES DIGESTION START?

IN ADULTS, THE DIGESTIVE SYSTEM IS ABOUT 9M (29FT) LONG! FOOD CAN TAKE ANYTHING FROM 10 TO 20 HOURS TO PASS THROUGH IT!

## • FACT FILE •

Almost no digestion occurs in the large intestine. The large intestine stores waste food products and absorbs water and small amounts of minerals. The waste materials that accumulate in the large intestine are roughage that cannot be digested in the body.

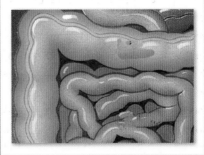

Digestion starts in the mouth. Chewing is very important for good digestion for two reasons. When chewed food is ground into fine particles, the digestive juices can act more easily. As the food is chewed, it is moistened and mixed with saliva, which contains the enzyme ptyalin. Ptyalin changes some of the starches in the food to sugar. After the food is swallowed, it passes through the oesophagus into the stomach.

The digestive juice in the stomach is called gastric juice. It contains hydrochloric acid and the enzyme pepsin. This juice begins the digestion of protein foods such as meat, eggs and milk. Starches, sugars and fats are not digested by the gastric juice. After a meal, some food remains in the stomach for two to five hours.

# WHAT TRAVELS DOWN THE ALIMENTARY CANAL?

The alimentary canal is a long tube through which food is taken into the body and digested. It begins at the mouth, and includes the pharynx, oesophagus, stomach, small and large intestines and rectum. When a person swallows food, the muscles of the pharynx push the food into the oesophagus.

The muscles in the oesophagus walls respond with a wave-like contraction called peristalsis. At the same time, the lower oesophageal sphincter relaxes, allowing the food to pass down to the stomach where digestion begins.

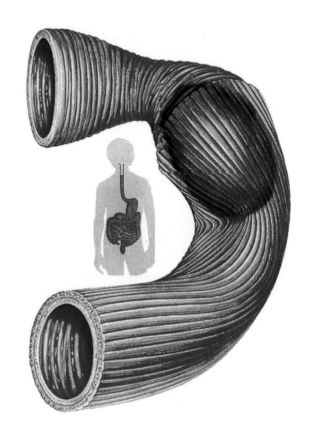

**IN HUMAN BEINGS, THE ALIMENTARY PASSAGE FROM PHARYNX TO RECTUM MEASURES ABOUT 9M (29FT) IN TOTAL!**

**FACT FILE**

The human oesophagus is about 25cm (10in) long. The length varies greatly in different animals. The oesophagus of a fish is short, while that of a giraffe is extremely long. Many birds have a saclike part of the oesophagus called the crop for temporary storage of food.

# WHERE WOULD YOU FIND THE EPIGLOTTIS?

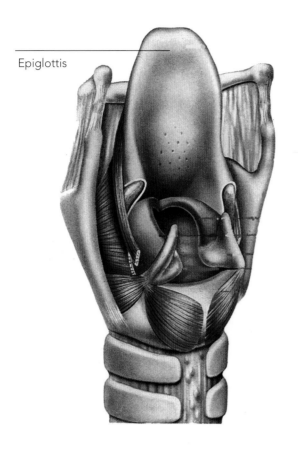

Epiglottis

The epiglottis is found in the throat. The throat is a term loosely applied to the part of the neck in front of the backbone. The throat contains structures important in breathing and eating. It includes the pharynx, the larynx, part of the oesophagus and part of the trachea.

Normally, when a person swallows, two actions take place to block off the air passage. The soft palate presses against the back of the pharynx, closing the opening to the nose. At the same time, the larynx rises and is covered by the epiglottis, a leaf-shaped lid.

These actions force the food into its own passage, the oesophagus, and muscular waves carry it on to the stomach.

**• FACT FILE •**

The thyroid is shaped like a bow tie under the skin of the neck. It manufactures three main hormones: calcitonin, which controls the level of calcium minerals in the blood and bones; thyroxine and tri-iodothyronine, which affect blood pressure and the speed of general body chemistry.

**?**

**DID YOU KNOW THAT THE LARYNX IS SOMETIMES CALLED THE VOICE BOX? THIS IS BECAUSE IT CONTAINS THE VOCAL CHORDS.**

# WHEN DO
# WE PRODUCE SALIVA?

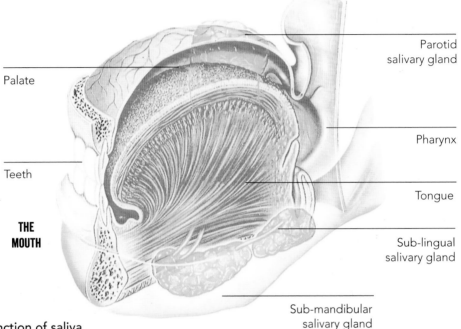

Palate

Teeth

**THE MOUTH**

Parotid salivary gland

Pharynx

Tongue

Sub-lingual salivary gland

Sub-mandibular salivary gland

The major function of saliva is to help in the process of digestion. It keeps the mouth moist and comfortable when we eat and helps to moisten dry food allowing it to be chewed and swallowed more easily. The mucus in saliva coats the bolus (or chewed food) and acts as a lubricant to help us to swallow.

The enzyme ptyalin which is found in saliva begins the first stage of digestion. It begins to break down starchy food into simpler sugars. Saliva also allows us to taste our food and drink. Each day each one of us produces about 1.7 litres (3pt) of saliva.

## • FACT FILE •

The four main tastes are sweet, salt, bitter and sour, and you can taste them with different parts of your tongue. You can check where the four tastes are by dabbing it with a little salt, sugar, coffee grounds (bitter) and lemon juice (sour).

Bitter

Sour

Salt

Sweet

# WHAT IS INSIDE THE STOMACH?

If you did not have a stomach you could not eat just two or three main meals each day. You would have to eat lots of tiny ones much more frequently. The stomach is like a stretchy storage bag for food. It expands to hold a whole meal. Then the layers of muscle in its walls contract to make it squeeze, first one way, then the other. Meanwhile, tiny glands in the stomach lining release their digestive chemicals, including powerful food-corroding acids and strong nutrient-splitting enzymes. Under this combined physical and chemical attack, after a few hours the food has become a mushy, part-digested soup. Around two to four hours after arriving in your stomach, the part-digested soup begins to leave. Small amounts trickle regularly from the stomach into the next section of the digestive tract – the small intestine.

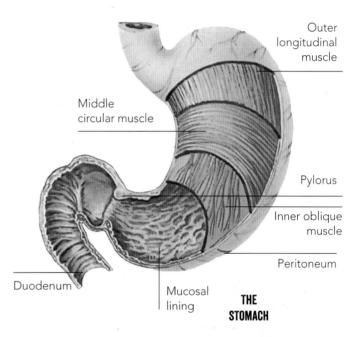

Outer longitudinal muscle

Middle circular muscle

Pylorus

Inner oblique muscle

Peritoneum

Duodenum

Mucosal lining

**THE STOMACH**

**AN ADULT STOMACH CAN HOLD AS MUCH AS 1.5 LITRES (2½PT) OF FOOD!**

**• FACT FILE •**

A normal X-ray photograph does not reveal the parts of the digestive system. However, a substance called barium shows up clearly on X-rays as a white area. If swallowed, this 'barium meal' can reveal problems such as ulcers, growths and blockages.

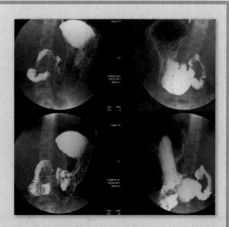

# WHEN DOES FOOD REACH OUR INTESTINES?

Everything you eat has to be chopped up and broken down before the nutrients or goodness in it can be taken into your blood and used by your body cells to make energy. This takes place in your digestive system or gut.

The food leaves your stomach a little at a time and goes into your small intestine. This is where most of the digestion takes place by adding digestive chemicals and absorbing the digested nutrients into the body. The lining of the intestine is folded into millions of tiny fingers called villi. Undigested food continues its journey on to the large intestine where excess water and minerals are extracted from the leftover food.

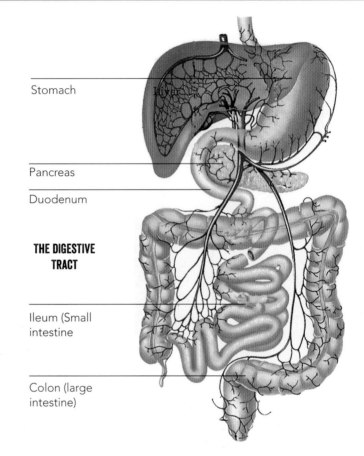

Stomach

Liver

Pancreas

Duodenum

**THE DIGESTIVE TRACT**

Ileum (Small intestine

Colon (large intestine)

How much energy do we use?

**Sitting or lying:**
43–72 calories per hour

**Walking:**
144–216 calories per hour

**Running:**
432–575 calories per hour

# WHERE IS THE DIGESTIVE PROCESS COMPLETED?

The digestive process is completed on the partly digested food in the small intestine, using pancreatic juice, intestinal juice and bile.

The pancreatic juice is produced by the pancreas and pours into the small intestine through a tube, or duct. The intestinal juice is produced by the walls of the small intestine. It has milder digestive effects than the pancreatic juice, but carries out similar digestion.

Bile is produced in the liver, stored in the gallbladder, and flows into the small intestine through the bile duct. When the food is completely digested, it is absorbed by tiny blood and lymph vessels in the walls of the small intestine. It is then carried into the circulation for nourishment of the body.

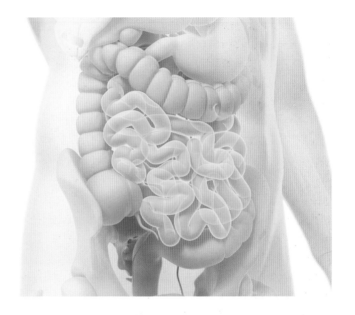

Food particles are small enough to pass through the walls of the intestine and blood vessels only when they are completely digested.

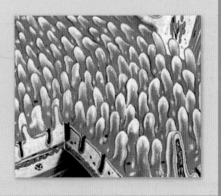

# WHAT IS THE PANCREAS?

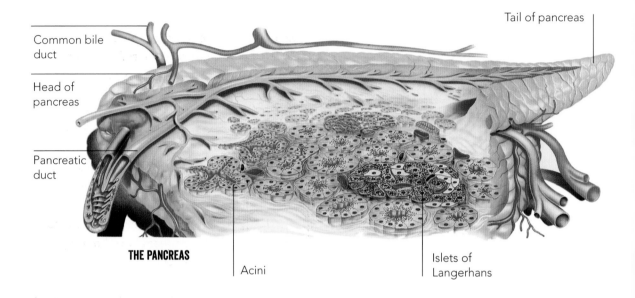

Tail of pancreas

Common bile duct

Head of pancreas

Pancreatic duct

**THE PANCREAS**

Acini

Islets of Langerhans

The pancreas is one of the largest glands in the body. Almost all of its cells are concerned with secretion. The pancreas lies across the upper part of the abdomen in front of the spine and on top of the aorta and the vena cava (the body's main artery and vein). The duodenum is wrapped round the head of the pancreas. The basic structures in the pancreas are the acini, which are collections of secreting cells around the end of a small duct. Each duct joins up with ducts from other acini until all of them eventually connect with the main duct running down the middle of the pancreas. The Islets of Langerhans are responsible for the secretion of insulin.

**The pancreas plays an important part in digestion as it secretes digestive enzymes into the small intestine.**

## FACT FILE

Are you frightened of spiders? When you are frightened or angry, your brain tells its hypothalamus area to send messages to your adrenal glands, which produce two 'emergency' hormones called adrenalin and noradrenalin.

# WHAT IS INSULIN?

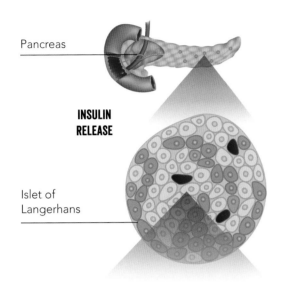

Pancreas

**INSULIN RELEASE**

Islet of Langerhans

Insulin is a hormone produced by the pancreas. The purpose of insulin is to keep the level of sugar in the blood down to normal levels. If the level of sugar in the blood begins to rise above certain limits, the Islets of Langerhans respond by releasing insulin into the bloodstream. The insulin then acts to oppose the effects of hormones such as cortisone and adrenalin, both of which raise the level of sugar in the blood. The insulin exerts its effect by allowing sugar to pass from the bloodstream into the body's cells to be used as a fuel.

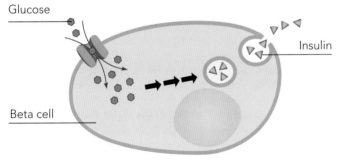

Glucose

Beta cell

Insulin

## • FACT FILE •

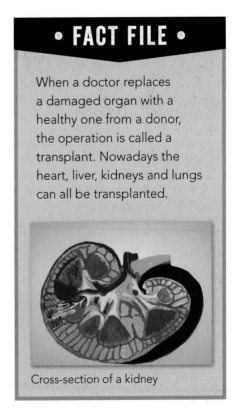

When a doctor replaces a damaged organ with a healthy one from a donor, the operation is called a transplant. Nowadays the heart, liver, kidneys and lungs can all be transplanted.

Cross-section of a kidney

**?** DID YOU KNOW SOME PEOPLE STOP BEING ABLE TO PRODUCE INSULIN? IT RESULTS IN A CONDITION CALLED TYPE 1 DIABETES, WHICH CAN BE FATAL IF NOT TREATED. PEOPLE WITH TYPE 1 DIABETES MUST TAKE DAILY INSULIN INJECTIONS IN ORDER TO SURVIVE.

# WHAT IS THE ROLE OF THE LIVER?

The liver is one of the body's busiest parts. It does not squirm about or move, like the stomach, intestines, heart or muscles. The liver's activities are invisible.

The liver is the body's largest inner organ and fills the top part of the abdomen, especially on the right side. The liver has a special blood vessel to it – the hepatic portal vein. This does not come directly from the heart, but carries blood that has been to the stomach, intestines and spleen. This blood is rich in nutrients, which provide the body with its energy and raw materials. The liver processes many of the nutrients brought to it by the blood. It stores others, especially glucose sugar, minerals such as iron, and vitamins such as B12. It also detoxifies a number of possibly harmful substances.

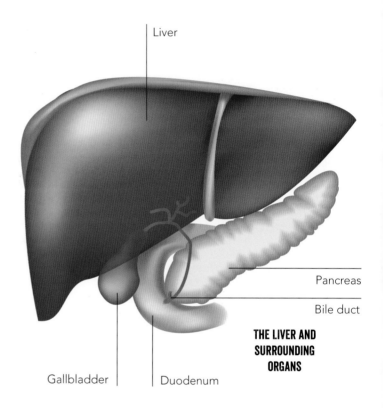

Liver

Pancreas

Bile duct

Gallbladder

Duodenum

**THE LIVER AND SURROUNDING ORGANS**

**THE LIVER HAS AT LEAST 500 KNOWN JOBS IN BODY CHEMISTRY, ALL DIFFERENT AND IMPORTANT!**

## FACT FILE

Cirrhosis of the liver is an irreversible chronic disease characterized by the replacement of functioning liver tissue with bands and lumps of scar tissue. This disease is often associated with drinking too much alcohol.

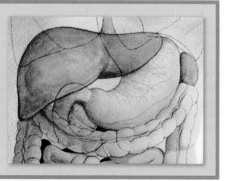

# WHEN MAY THE LIVER FAIL TO FUNCTION PROPERLY?

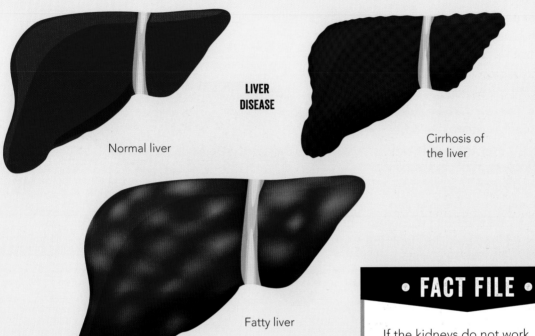

**LIVER DISEASE**

Normal liver

Cirrhosis of the liver

Fatty liver

The liver has two vital roles to play: making (or processing) new chemicals, and neutralizing poisons and waste products. The liver is the largest organ in the body weighing between 1.36 and 1.81kg (3 and 4lb). It is only possible for the blood to get back to the heart and lungs from the stomach by first passing through a system of veins in the liver, known as the portal system.

A variety of things including viruses, drugs, environmental pollutants, genetic disorders and systemic diseases can affect the liver and stop it functioning properly. However, the liver has a marvellous capacity to renew itself and will usually return to normal once the causes are removed or eliminated.

## • FACT FILE •

If the kidneys do not work properly, they can become 'furred' up with hard crusts and crystals of chemicals from the urine. These deposits are called kidney stones. They can be removed by an operation, dissolved by drugs, or shattered into tiny fragments by ultrasonic sound waves.

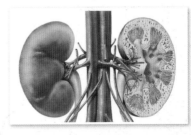

# WHAT IS THE CIRCULATORY STRUCTURE OF THE LIVER?

The liver performs more separate tasks than any other organ in the body. Its chief functions are to help the body digest and use food and to help purify the blood of wastes and poisons. The liver has an unusual blood supply system. Like other organs, the liver receives blood containing oxygen from the heart. This blood enters the liver through the hepatic artery. The liver also receives blood filled with nutrients, or digested food particles, from the small intestine. This blood enters the liver through the portal vein. In the liver, the hepatic artery and the portal vein branch into a network of tiny blood vessels.

The liver cells absorb nutrients and oxygen from the blood as it flows through the blood vessels. They also filter out wastes and poisons. At the same time, they secrete

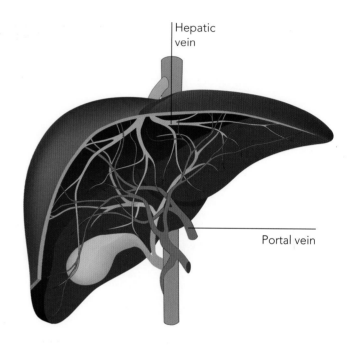

Hepatic vein

Portal vein

sugar, vitamins, minerals and other substances into the blood. The blood vessels drain into the central veins, which join to form the hepatic vein. Blood leaves the liver through the hepatic vein.

## FACT FILE

The liver plays an essential role in the storage of certain vitamins. The liver stores vitamin A, as well as vitamins D, E and K and those of the B-complex group. It also stores iron and other minerals.

# WHERE DOES THE BODY STORE BILE?

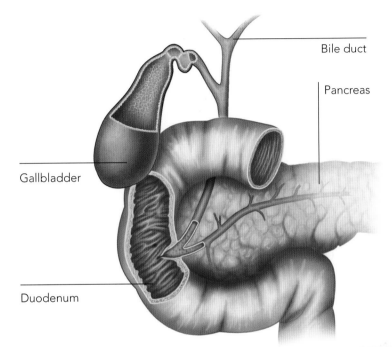

Bile duct

Pancreas

Gallbladder

Duodenum

**THE GALLBLADDER CAN HOLD ABOUT 44ML (1½FL OZ) OF BILE AT ANY ONE TIME!**

Bile is stored in a small pouch called the gallbladder, a pear-shaped sac that rests on the underside of the right portion of the liver. The neck of the gallbladder connects with the cystic duct, which enters the hepatic duct, a tube from the liver. Together, these two tubes form the common bile duct.

During digestion, bile flows from the liver through the hepatic duct into the common bile duct and empties into the duodenum, which is the first section of the small intestine. Between meals, the bile is not needed but it continues to flow from the liver into the common bile duct. It is kept out of the duodenum by a small, ring-like muscle called the sphincter of Oddi, which tightens around the opening. The fluid is then forced to flow into the gallbladder, where it is concentrated and stored until it is needed for digestion.

## • FACT FILE •

Sometimes the gallbladder becomes filled with hard lumps, on average about the size of a pea. They are made from various substances, chiefly cholesterol and calcium. They can be removed by surgery or smashed into tiny pieces by very high-pitched sound waves called ultrasound.

# WHAT IS THE ROLE OF THE KIDNEYS?

Our bodies' cells 'burn' nutrients and oxygen to make energy to live and grow, in much the same way that wood and other materials are burnt to produce another sort of energy – heat. But just as fires produce waste gases and ash, so the 'burning' that takes place in our body cells also creates waste products. These must be removed, or they would poison us.

The removal of these waste materials is known as excretion, and the body's main organs of excretion are the kidneys. You have two kidneys positioned in the small of your back, one on either side of your backbone. They look like large reddish-brown beans and each one is about the size of a clenched fist. Kidneys clean the blood by filtering out waste materials and straining off any water the body doesn't need. This liquid waste is called urine. It is stored in your bladder and then leaves your body when you go to the toilet.

Human kidneys consist of three layers. These layers are, in order, the cortex on the outside of the organ, the medulla and the pelvis. Blood flows into the medulla through the renal artery. In the medulla and cortex, the renal artery branches into increasingly smaller arteries. Each of these arteries ends in a blood filtration unit called a nephron, which filters out unwanted salts, urea and water – urine.

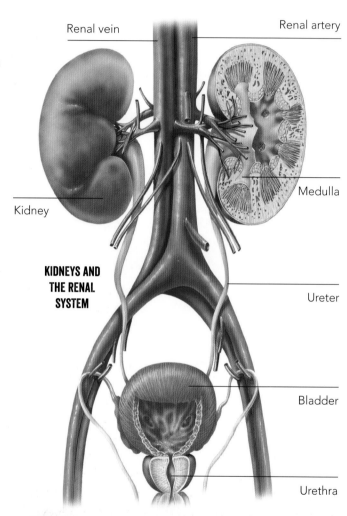

Renal vein

Renal artery

Kidney

Medulla

**KIDNEYS AND THE RENAL SYSTEM**

Ureter

Bladder

Urethra

## FACT FILE

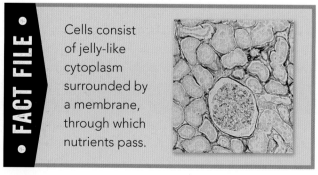

Cells consist of jelly-like cytoplasm surrounded by a membrane, through which nutrients pass.

# WHAT IS DIALYSIS?

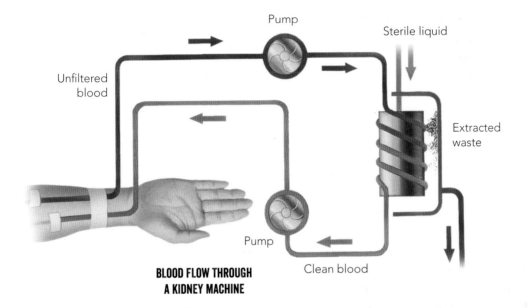

Pump

Sterile liquid

Unfiltered blood

Extracted waste

Pump

Clean blood

**BLOOD FLOW THROUGH A KIDNEY MACHINE**

If the kidneys become diseased and stop working, it is necessary to use a kidney machine to remove waste products from the blood. This process is called dialysis. It involves pumping blood from a tube in the person's arm into thin tubing that runs through a tank of sterile liquid. Waste passes from the blood through the walls of the tubing, and the cleaned blood is returned to the body. The dialysis machine works in the same way as the two main blood vessels running to and from the kidneys. One tube takes the unfiltered blood from the body (like the renal artery), while another tube takes the cleaned blood back into the body (like the renal vein). This process has to be done throughout the person's life, unless a new kidney can be provided in a transplant operation. Dialysis needs to be carried out frequently, several times a week, to stop wastes from building up to a dangerous level.

## • FACT FILE •

The human body is made up of approximately 70 per cent water. It is therefore very important that we drink plenty of water every day.

# WHERE WOULD YOU FIND NEPHRONS?

Nephrons are found in the kidneys; they are the millions of tiny filtering units that clean your blood. The renal artery brings unfiltered blood to the kidneys. It branches into over one million capillaries inside each kidney. Each capillary is twisted into a knot called the glomerulus, which is enclosed by a structure called a Bowman's capsule.

Blood is cleaned as it filters through the capsule and the tubule attached to it. The clean blood then passes back into the capillaries, which join up into the renal vein.

Urine continues down the tubule, which joins up with other tubules to form the ureter. The ureter then leads to the bladder.

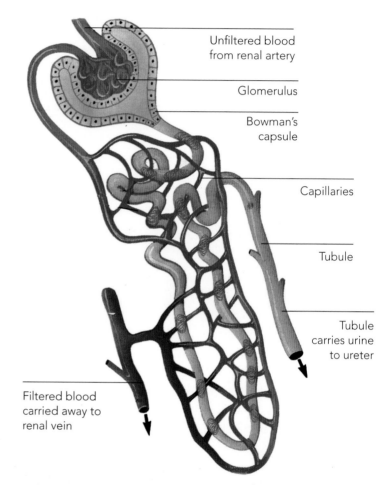

Unfiltered blood from renal artery

Glomerulus

Bowman's capsule

Capillaries

Tubule

Tubule carries urine to ureter

Filtered blood carried away to renal vein

## FACT FILE

The two kidneys perform many vital functions, of which the most important is the production of urine.

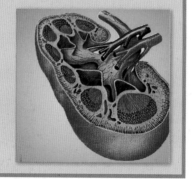

TWO HEALTHY KIDNEYS CONTAIN A TOTAL OF ABOUT TWO MILLION NEPHRONS, WHICH FILTER ABOUT 1,900L (500 GALLONS) OF BLOOD DAILY!

# WHERE IS URINE STORED?

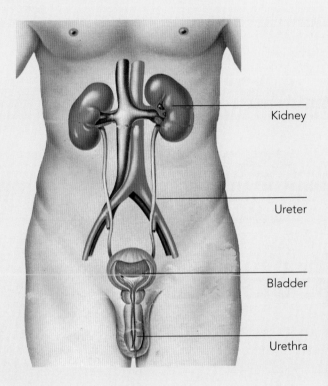

Kidney

Ureter

Bladder

Urethra

**The bladder lies just behind the pubis, one of the bones of the pelvis.**

The bladder is the common name for the urinary bladder, a hollow muscular organ that stores urine before expelling it from the body. The emptying of the urinary bladder is voluntarily controlled in most human beings and many other mammals.

Urine drains continuously from the kidneys into the bladder through two tubes called ureters. It leaves the bladder through the urethra, a wider tube that leads out of the body. The place where the bladder and the urethra meet is called the neck of the bladder. A complex arrangement of muscles encircles the bladder neck. This ring, called the urethral sphincter, normally prevents urine from leaving the bladder. The bladder can hold more than ½ litre (1pt) of urine.

## • FACT FILE •

We lose around 3 litres (5pt) of water a day through our skin as sweat, and in our breath and urine. We also get rid of extra salt in sweat and we expel waste carbon dioxide gas when we breathe out.

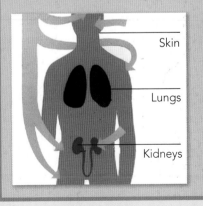

Skin

Lungs

Kidneys

# THE SENSES

# CONTENTS

# HOW DO OUR EYES WORK?

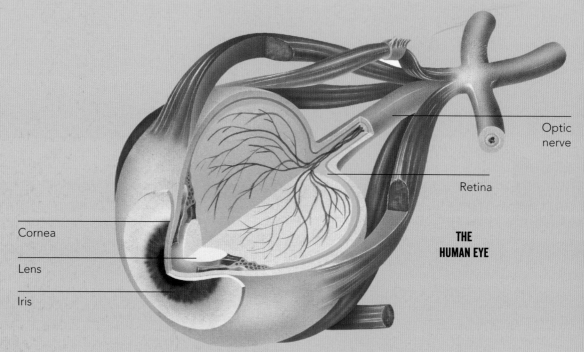

Optic nerve

Retina

Cornea

Lens

Iris

**THE HUMAN EYE**

The eye is very like a camera. It has an adjustable opening to let in the light (the pupil), a lens that focuses the light to form an image and a sensitive film (the retina) on which the image is recorded.

Inside each human eye are about 130,000,000 light-sensitive cells. When light falls on one of these cells it causes a chemical change. This change starts an impulse in the eye fibre, which sends a message through the optic nerve to the 'seeing' part of your brain. The brain has learned what this message means so that we know exactly what we are seeing.

The eye itself is shaped like a ball with a slight bulge at the front. In the middle is a hole called the 'pupil', which appears black because it opens into the dark inside of the eye. Light passes through the pupil to the lens. The lens then focuses the light forming a picture at the back of the eyeball.

## • FACT FILE •

People with normal vision will be able to see three shapes in this diagram. Those who are colour-blind will only be able to see coloured dots.

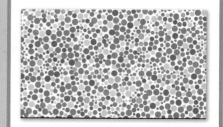

# HOW DO
# I SEE IN COLOUR?

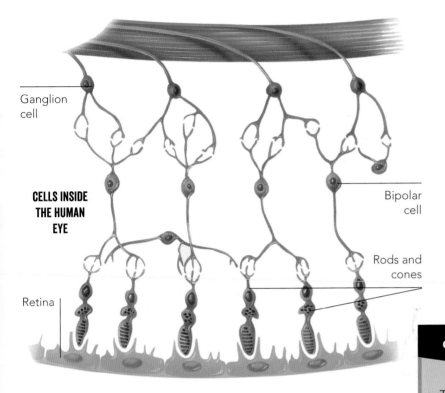

Ganglion cell

CELLS INSIDE THE HUMAN EYE

Bipolar cell

Rods and cones

Retina

EACH OF YOUR EYES HAS 125 MILLION ROD CELLS AND 7 MILLION CONE CELLS! THEY ARE ATTACHED TO NERVES IN ORDER TO PASS ON INFORMATION AS THEY DETECT LIGHT WHEN IT FALLS ON THEM.

The retina is filled with a layer of tiny cells called rods and cones. These cells contain coloured substances that react when light falls on them, triggering a nerve impulse.

Rods are slim cells that are responsible for us seeing in black and white. They work even if the light is very poor, when we see everything in shades of grey.

Cone cells give us colour vision. They contain different light-sensitive substances that respond to either red, yellow-green or blue-violet light. Together with the grey images produced from the rods, cone cells produce the coloured picture that you see.

Cones can only work in bright light, which is why colours are so hard to see in dim light.

## • FACT FILE •

True colour blindness is when people cannot see any colour at all, but this is very rare. The most common form is red-green colour blindness, where people find it difficult to distinguish between red, green and brown.

# WHAT IS THE RETINA?

When light rays have passed through the cornea and lens in the eye, they shine onto the rear inner surface of the eyeball, a layer called the retina. It is not much bigger than a postage stamp, and even thinner. Yet it contains more than 130 million microscopic cells. When light shines on them, they generate nerve signals – that is, they are light sensitive. There are two types of light-sensitive cells in the retina, named after their shapes – rods and cones. There are about 125 million rods and they all respond to all types of light, regardless of whether it is white, red, blue, green or yellow. Rods work in very weak light, so they help the eye to see in dim conditions. The other type of light-sensitive cell is the cone. There are about seven million of them in the retina, clustered mainly around the back, opposite the lens.

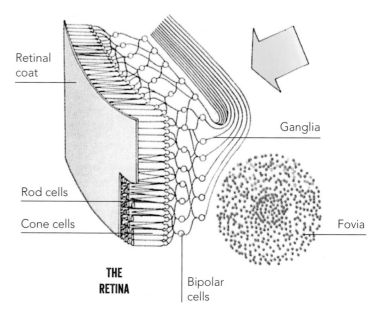

Retinal coat

Ganglia

Rod cells

Cone cells

Fovia

**THE RETINA**

Bipolar cells

## FACT FILE

The image of the world 'lingers' for a fraction of a second on the retina and in the brain. This means if images change very fast, each merges or blurs into the next, so we see them as one smooth, continuous moving scene.

# WHAT MAKES
# THE EYEBALL MOVE?

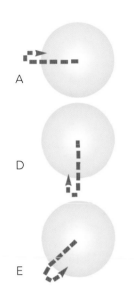

A

D

E

Superior oblique

Superior rectus

Optic nerve

Medial rectus

Lateral rectus

Inferior oblique

Inferior rectus

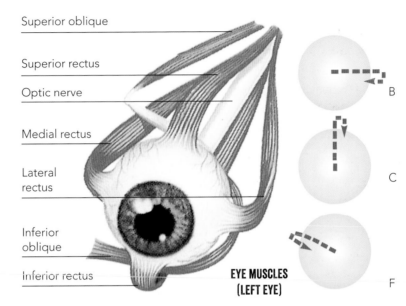

**EYE MUSCLES
(LEFT EYE)**

B

C

F

There are six muscles to control the movements of each eye. Muscle (A) swivels it away from the nose; (B) towards the nose; (C) rotates it upwards; (D) downwards; (E) moves it down and outwards and (F) moves it upwards and outwards.

All these movements are coordinated in the brain. If the lateral rectus muscle in one eye contracts, the medial rectus of the other will contract to a similar extent. The superior recti work together to pull the eyes back and also to look up. The inferior recti make the eyes look down. The superior oblique muscles rotate the eye downwards and outwards and the inferior oblique upwards and outwards.

## • FACT FILE •

The eyes are the body's windows on the world and need special protection. Every second or so the eyelids blink and sweep tear fluid across the eye washing away dust and germs. Eyebrows stop water from dripping down into the eyes. Eyelashes help to keep out the dust.

# WHAT IS PUPIL REFLEX?

The muscles contract to make the pupil smaller in bright conditions. This stops too much light getting into the eye and damaging its delicate inner parts.

The retina is very sensitive to light. Too much light (A) distorts what we see and is dazzling. The pupils vary in size and thus reduce or increase the amount of light entering the eye. Bright light causes a reflex nervous reaction, controlled by areas in the midbrain. The circular pupillary muscle (1) in both irises contracts and the radial strands (2) extend, thus narrowing the diameter. Poor light (B) will make both pupils dilate, allowing sufficient light to stimulate the cells in the retina (3).

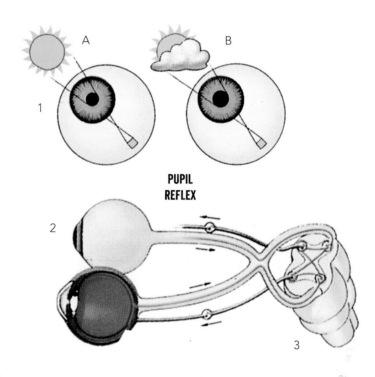

**PUPIL REFLEX**

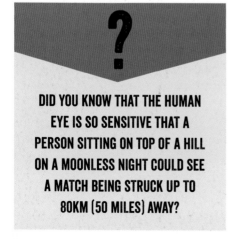

**DID YOU KNOW THAT THE HUMAN EYE IS SO SENSITIVE THAT A PERSON SITTING ON TOP OF A HILL ON A MOONLESS NIGHT COULD SEE A MATCH BEING STRUCK UP TO 80KM (50 MILES) AWAY?**

**• FACT FILE •**

Birds have the keenest sight of all animals, including human beings. An osprey (right) can see a dead animal on the ground from a height of up to 4km (2½ miles).

# WHAT IS THE FOCUSING MECHANISM IN THE EYE?

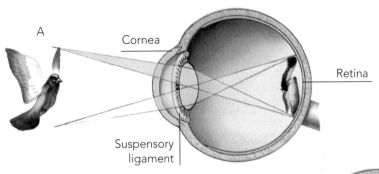

A

Cornea

Retina

Suspensory ligament

**FOCUSING MECHANISM**

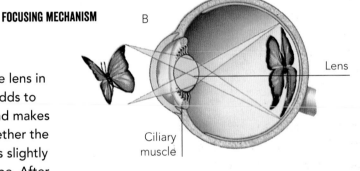

B

Lens

Ciliary muscle

The lens of the eye is shaped like the lens in a camera and does a similar job. It adds to the focusing power of the cornea and makes fine adjustments, depending on whether the object is near or far. The eye's lens is slightly elastic and focuses by changing shape. After passing through the lens, the light rays go through the clear jelly in the middle of the eyeball to the retina. In distant vision (A) the muscles relax and the ligaments pull the lens into a disc shape. Close vision (B) requires a more circular lens, so the muscles constrict and the ligaments relax.

**?**

DID YOU KNOW THAT THE IMAGE THAT FORMS ON THE RETINA WHEN LIGHT PASSES THROUGH THE LENS IS ACTUALLY UPSIDE DOWN? THIS IS BECAUSE OF THE WAY IN WHICH LIGHT RAYS ARE BENT BY THE EYE'S LENS. THE BRAIN AUTOMATICALLY TURNS THE IMAGE THE RIGHT WAY UP.

## • FACT FILE •

Why do we have two eyes? Close one eye. Hold a pencil in one hand. Stretch out your arm in front of you and try to touch something. Can you do it? Two eyes working together help you to see how close things really are.

# WHAT PURPOSE DO TEARS SERVE?

Tears are the secretion of the lacrimal glands. They continually bathe the cornea, the tough outer layer of the eyeball. They help to clear it of foreign particles, such as dust and hairs, and keep it from drying out, which would result in blindness. Two lacrimal glands, one over each eye, lie behind the eyelid. They pour out their fluid through several small ducts in the underside of the eyelid. Each time a person blinks an eyelid, it sucks a little fluid from the glands. When a person feels some emotion very strongly, such as grief or anger, the muscles around the lacrimal glands may tighten up and squeeze out the tear fluid. The same thing happens if a person laughs very heartily. After the tears pass across the eyeball, they flow out through two lacrimal ducts that open at the inner corner of each eye.

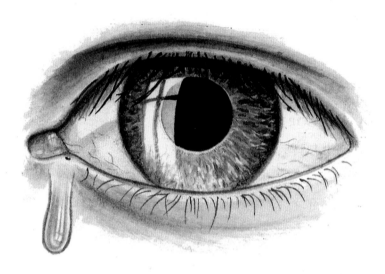

After crying, a person may have to blow their nose to clear the drainage system of excess tears.

## • FACT FILE •

Mostly a salt solution, lacrimal fluid also contains substances that fight bacteria, and proteins that help make the eye immune to infection.

# WHY DO SOME PEOPLE WEAR GLASSES OR CONTACT LENSES?

If the eye is not exactly the right shape, or the lens cannot focus properly, you cannot form a clear image on the retina. In this case you may need to wear glasses to correct your vision. For a short-sighted person, distant object look blurred because the image forms in front of the retina. A short-sighted person can see nearby objects very clearly. For a long-sighted person, the image tries to form behind the retina, so it is blurred while the lens tries to focus on a nearby object.

Contact lenses are an alternative to wearing glasses and many people prefer these. They are thin plastic discs that rest on the surface of the cornea. They act like the lenses of ordinary glasses. Most modern contact lenses are made from very soft material that does not cause any discomfort to the eye. Some lenses are only worn for just one day and then they are thrown away.

**?**

DID YOU KNOW THAT, AS PEOPLE GET OLDER, THE LENSES OF THEIR EYES GROW HARDER AND CANNOT CHANGE THEIR SHAPE TO FOCUS CLOSE UP?

# WHAT IS INSIDE THE EAR?

Hearing involves much more than the ears on the side of your head. These are the outer ears or ear flaps, made of skin-covered cartilage. The ear is actually made up of three parts. The outer ear collects sound waves, which are vibrations in the air. The middle ear turns them into vibrations in solids – the ear drum and tiny bones. The inner ear changes them into vibrations in fluid, and then into electrical nerve signals. The inner ear also gives us our sense of balance. The middle and inner ears are protected from knocks by skull bones. The hairs and waxy lining of the outer ear canal gather and remove dust and germs.

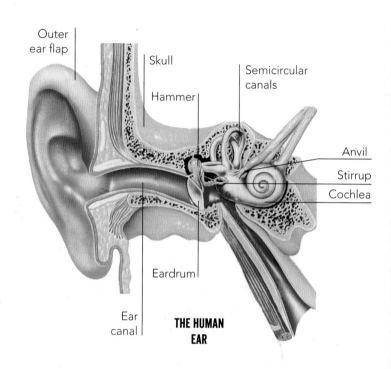

Outer ear flap

Skull

Hammer

Semicircular canals

Anvil

Stirrup

Cochlea

Eardrum

Ear canal

**THE HUMAN EAR**

The middle and inner ears are protected from knocks by skull bones.

# HOW DO WE HEAR?

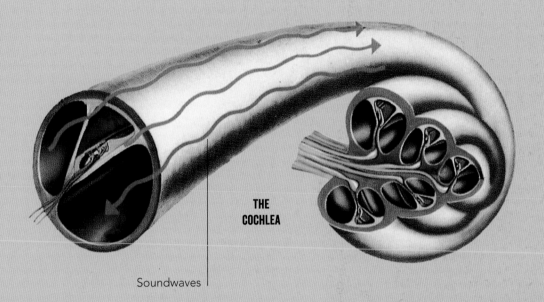

THE
COCHLEA

Soundwaves

The hearing portion is situated at one end of the ear chamber and forms a coil rather like the shell of a snail. It is called the cochlea and throughout its length runs a thin membrane called the basilar membrane, which supplies thousands of tiny nerve threads to the cochlea nerve. Changes in the pitch or loudness of sounds are sensed by tiny hairs through which pressure waves travel.

When sounds travel into the ear, they make the eardrum inside vibrate, or shake. The vibrations pass along a chain of tiny bones called the hammer, anvil and stirrup, and are made louder before passing into the cochlea.

The vibrations are then picked up by nerve endings inside the cochlea, and changed into messages to send to the brain.

# HOW SENSITIVE IS MY HEARING?

Sound is measured in decibels (dB). We can hear sounds ranging from a low rumble up to a high-pitched whistle. The lowest sounds can sometimes be felt in the chest, while very shrill sounds may be so high that we cannot actually hear them.

A bat's squeak is at the limit of what human beings can hear, and many people cannot hear this noise at all. Our hearing is not very sensitive compared to animals such as dogs, who can hear very high-pitched sounds. Dogs are able to respond to a supersonic whistle that cannot be heard by humans at all.

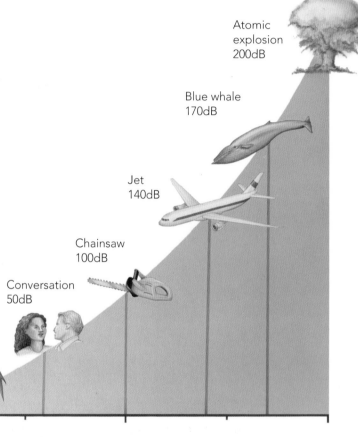

Atomic explosion 200dB

Blue whale 170dB

Jet 140dB

Chainsaw 100dB

Conversation 50dB

Birdsong 30dB

**THE RELATIVE DECIBEL SCALE**

# HOW DO DEAF PEOPLE COMMUNICATE?

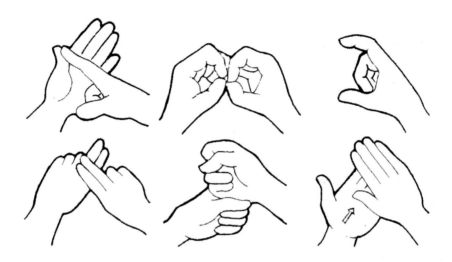

Many people who are deaf or hard of hearing use speech reading and manual communication to help them communicate. Speech reading, also called lip reading, involves understanding what is said by watching the movements of the speaker's mouth, face and body. In manual communication, people talk primarily with their hands. Manual communication usually involves both finger spelling and sign languages. In finger spelling, a different hand signal represents each letter of the alphabet. In sign languages, hand signals stand for objects and ideas. Sign languages are used throughout the world in the same rich variety as spoken languages. Deaf people use manual communication to converse with people who understand finger spelling and sign language.

# HOW DO WE SMELL?

Our sense of smell is probably the oldest of the five senses. As you breathe in, air passes through a cavity behind the nose, which contains patches of millions of smell receptors called olfactory cells. Sensory hairs stick out from the surface of these receptor cells and these hairs detect smells and pass information along nerve fibres to the brain. Substances that you can recognize as having an odour dissolve in the layer of mucus covering the sensory cells, stimulating them to produce a signal. Most people are able to detect about 4,000 different smells. However, people whose work is based on their ability to smell, such as chefs, perfume makers and wine tasters, can distinguish as many as 10,000 different smells.

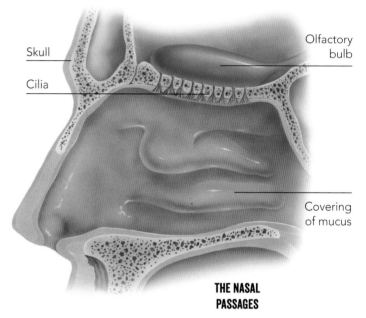

Skull

Cilia

Olfactory bulb

Covering of mucus

**THE NASAL PASSAGES**

IT HAS BEEN ESTIMATED THAT A PERSON NEEDS 25,000 TIMES AS MUCH OF A SUBSTANCE IN THE MOUTH TO TASTE IT AS IS NEEDED BY THE SMELL RECEPTORS TO SMELL IT!

**• FACT FILE •**

The sense of smell in dogs is very highly developed. 'Sniffer' dogs are often used to find people buried under an avalanche or in houses destroyed by earthquakes. They are also trained to sniff out drugs and work in conjunction with the police.

# HOW DO
# WE TASTE THINGS?

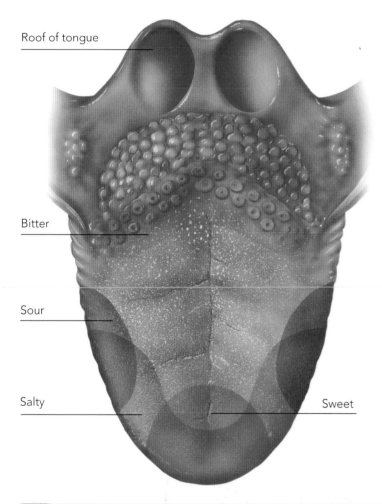

Roof of tongue

Bitter

Sour

Salty

Sweet

There are distinct regions on the tongue where the main tastes are recognized. The tongue is covered with small bumps, called taste buds, which are grouped together in areas with different functions. These taste buds react to simple tastes and pass messages to the brain.

The taste buds, or 'flavour receptors', transmit the different taste information as a message to the brain. It is the brain that processes the information and tells us what food is actually in our mouths. As we grow older our taste buds become less sensitive. This is one of the reasons why elderly people may no longer enjoy their food so much. Hot foods taste better because the heat causes more of the pleasant smells to rise into the nose. These abundant smells contribute to the total taste of the food.

**WE EACH HAVE AROUND 10,000 TASTE BUDS ON OUR TONGUES!**

# HOW DO
# TASTE BUDS WORK?

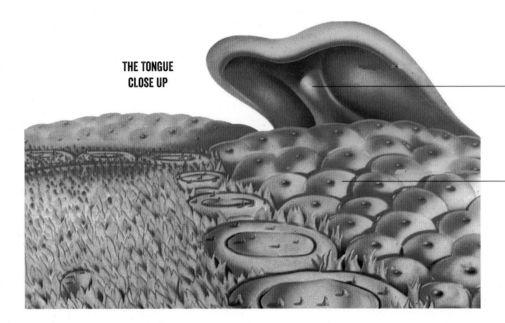

**THE TONGUE CLOSE UP**

Epiglottis

Papillae

Taste buds are found within the papillae that cover the surface of the tongue.

Tastes are detected by thousands of taste buds scattered along the tip, sides and back of the tongue. Each taste bud is tiny – a microscopic bunch of about 50 cells that have frilly tips. There are four main types of taste: sweet, sour, salty and bitter. A fifth taste – umami – has also been recognized in recent years, and relates to the Japanese word for savoury. When molecules land on the frilly tip, the taste-bud cells make nerve signals. These pass along small nerves, which gather into two main nerves – the seventh and ninth cranial nerves. These signals then travel along them to the taste area in the brain.

**The chief organ of taste, the tongue also helps in chewing and swallowing, and plays an important part in forming the sounds of words.**

## • FACT FILE •

The surface of the tongue is rough, thanks to the many small projections called papillae. Each papilla contains 100–200 taste buds.

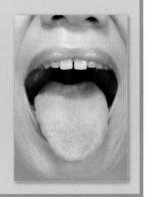

# HOW SIMILAR ARE TASTE AND SMELL?

An Indian thali

When we taste food it is a mixture of both taste and smell. As you eat, tiny food particles drift up into the passages of the nose from the back of the mouth.

The smell of the food contributes to the simple tastes detected by the tongue. This explains why food tastes odd when we have a cold because the nasal organs become inflamed and therefore the sense of smell is temporarily smothered.

When we eat spicy foods, such as curry or chilli, mild pain also forms a part of the characteristic taste. If these foods did not burn the mouth slightly, they would not taste like curry or chilli at all. If we were to lose our sense of smell, almost all taste sensation would be lost as well, meaning that we would not enjoy the taste of our food nearly so much.

## • FACT FILE •

When we sneeze, a cloud of tiny water droplets is ejected violently through the mouth and nose carrying with it any microbes present in your lungs. This is how colds and influenza are spread.

# WHY IS TOUCH AN IMPORTANT SENSE?

Your skin is continuously passing huge amounts of information to your brain. It monitors touch, pain, temperature and other factors that tell the brain exactly how the body is being affected by its environment. Without this constant flow of information you would keep injuring yourself accidentally. You would be unable to sense whether something was very hot, very cold, very sharp, very rough, and so on. In some rare diseases the skin senses are lost and these people have to be very careful so that they don't cause themselves harm.

Tiny sensory receptors in the skin provide our sense of touch. They measure touch, pressure, pain, heat and cold and keep the brain updated about the state of the environment.

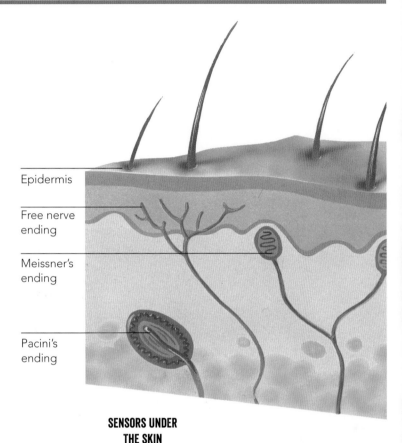

Epidermis

Free nerve ending

Meissner's ending

Pacini's ending

**SENSORS UNDER THE SKIN**

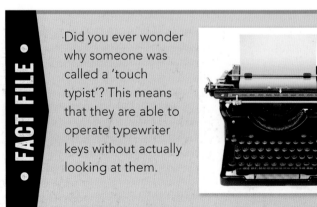

# WHY ARE SOME BODY PARTS MORE SENSITIVE THAN OTHERS?

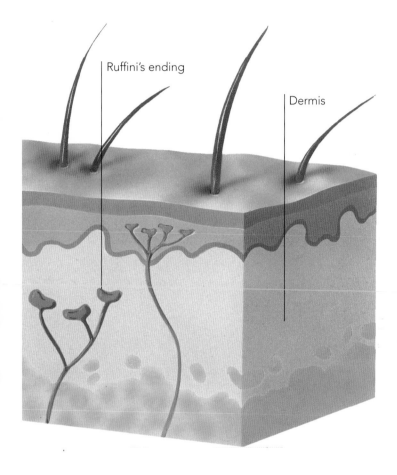

Ruffini's ending

Dermis

Sensations in the skin are measured by tiny receptors at the ends of nerve fibres.

There are several different types of receptor. Each type can detect only one kind of sensation, such as pain, temperature, pressure, touch and so on.

These receptors are grouped together according to the importance of their function. There are large numbers in the hands and lips, for example, where the sensation of touch is very important. Your back, however, is far less sensitive as there are fewer receptors in that area of your body.

Receptor types include: Ruffini's nerve ending, which detects sustained pressure; Meissner's nerve ending, which detects changes in texture and slow vibrations; Pacini's nerve ending, which detects prolonged touch.

**FACT FILE**

The hands are among the body's most sensitive parts. The fingertips are especially sensitive. On one hand there are millions of nerve-endings.

# HAIR, SKIN AND TEETH

# CONTENTS

# WHAT'S INSIDE A TOOTH?

A tooth consists of four different kinds of tissue. These are pulp, dentine, enamel and cementum.

Pulp is the innermost layer of a tooth. It consists of connective tissue, blood vessels and nerves. The blood vessels nourish the tooth. The nerves transmit sensations of pain to the brain.

Dentine is a hard, yellow substance that surrounds the pulp. It makes up most of a tooth. Dentine is harder than bone. It consists mainly of mineral salts and water but also has some living cells.

Enamel overlays the dentine in the crown of the tooth. It forms the outermost covering of the crown. Enamel is the hardest tissue in the body. It enables a tooth to withstand the pressure placed on it during chewing. Cementum overlays the dentine in the root of the tooth. In most cases, the cementum and enamel meet where the root ends and the crown begins. As the surface of the tooth wears away, the tooth grows further out of its socket, exposing the root.

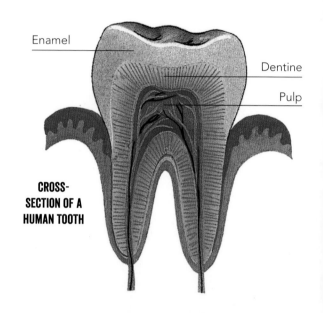

Enamel

Dentine

Pulp

**CROSS-SECTION OF A HUMAN TOOTH**

### • FACT FILE •

Sometimes teeth grow crookedly or become overcrowded in the mouth. This can be put right by wearing teeth braces. Braces consist of metal or clear – sometimes coloured -- ceramic brackets that are bonded onto the front surface of each tooth and connected by wires.

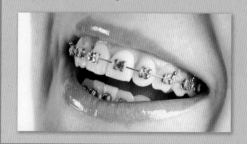

**?**

**DID YOU KNOW THAT THE AVERAGE PERSON SPENDS AROUND 35 DAYS OF THEIR ENTIRE LIFETIME BRUSHING THEIR TEETH?**

# HOW DO TEETH DIFFER?

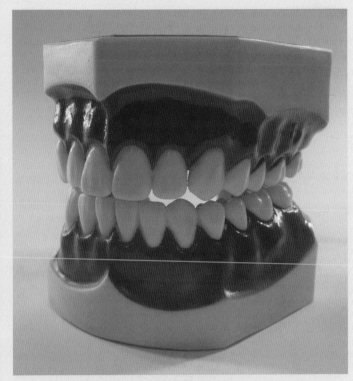

Dental model of human teeth

Your first set of teeth are called milk teeth. These teeth grow beneath the gum and have to force their way out. This process is called teething, and can be very painful. You only have 20 milk teeth.

Later another set of teeth form in the gum, under the first set. This second set of teeth gradually pushes the milk teeth out until there are 32 permanent teeth.

Teeth have different shapes so that they can carry out different jobs. Incisor teeth at the front of the mouth are flat and shaped like chisels. You use them to cut your food. The canines are the pointed teeth just behind the incisors, and you use them to tear food.

The back teeth, called molars and premolars, are flattened so they can grind the food into small pieces ready for swallowing.

Wisdom teeth are a mystery as no-one has discovered exactly why humans have them.

## • FACT FILE •

Babies are usually born without teeth, as they survive on only milk for the first few months of their lives.

 **NO TWO SETS OF TEETH ARE THE SAME – YOUR TEETH ARE AS UNIQUE AS YOUR FINGERPRINTS!**

# WHEN DO
# WE LOSE OUR MILK TEETH?

The average person has two sets of teeth, one after the other. The first is the baby, milk, or deciduous set. Even before birth, teeth appear as tiny buds below the gums. They begin to erupt, or show above the gum from the age of a few months. By the age of about three all 20 first teeth have usually appeared. In each half (left and right) of each jaw (upper and lower), there are two incisors, one canine and two molars.

From about the age of six years, the first teeth start to fall out. These are replaced by the adult, second, or permanent set. First are usually the front incisors and the first molars, at around seven to eight years. Last are the rear-most molars, or wisdom teeth. They appear at 18–20 years of age in some people, while in others they erupt at 40 or 50 years of age – and sometimes they never appear. In each half of each jaw, there are typically two incisors, one canine, two premolars, and three molars, making a full set of 32 teeth.

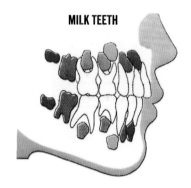

MILK TEETH

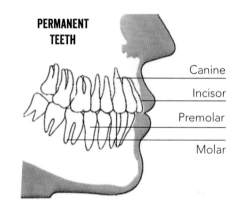

PERMANENT TEETH

Canine

Incisor

Premolar

Molar

Although babies are born without teeth, they have already started to grow beneath the gums – this starts while a baby is still in the womb.

**• FACT FILE •**

Your back teeth are bumpy on top. You can feel it. They work together, grinding food between the bumps. These grinders need regular and careful cleaning when they finish work, as food often sticks between the bumps.

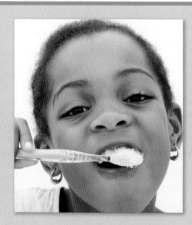

# HOW FAST DOES HAIR GROW?

**HAIR IS MADE UP OF THE SAME SUBSTANCE THAT MAKES A HORSE'S HOOVES AND CATS' CLAWS! IT IS CALLED KERATIN.**

For men who are becoming a little bald, hair doesn't grow fast enough! But in the case of a young boy, the hair seems to grow too fast! The rate at which hair grows has actually been measured and found to be about 1.5cm (½in) a month. The hair doesn't grow at the same rate throughout the day but seems to follow a kind of rhythm. At night, the hair grows slowly, but as day begins, this is speeded up. Between 10 and 11am, the speed of growth is at its greatest. Then the hair grows slowly again. It picks up speed between 4 and 6pm, and then the growing slows up again.

Of course, these variations in the speed of growth are so tiny that you cannot possibly notice them. So don't expect to stand in front of the mirror at 10am and be able to watch your hair sprouting up! Not all people have the same amount of hair. Blonde people tend to have finer hair, but more profuse than dark people. Red-haired people have the coarsest and fewest hairs.

## • FACT FILE •

The custom of shaving was introduced to England by the Saxons. Barbers first appeared in Roman times in 300 BCE. Nowadays, there is a great variety of facial hair-styles from beards and moustaches to the clean-shaven effect.

# WHAT MAKES HAIR CURLY?

Skin feels smooth, but under a microscope it looks like a jagged mountain range with huge pits of sprouting hair.

These pits are called follicles, and they make hair straight or curly. Straight hair grows from a round follicle (1), wavy hair grows from an oval-shaped one (2), and very curly hair grows from a flat one (3).

The texture of hair depends largely on the shape of the hair, which can be seen in cross-section under a microscope. Straight hairs have a round shape, and wavy and curly hairs are flat. The flattest hairs are the waviest or curliest.

The number of hairs you have on your head depends on the colour of your hair. Most blondes have about 140,000 head hairs, redheads average 90,000, while people with black or brown hair come somewhere in the middle with about 110,000 hairs.

Most hair follicles contain an oil gland called the sebaceous gland. This gland secretes oil into the follicle. The oil flows over the hair, lubricating it and keeping it soft.

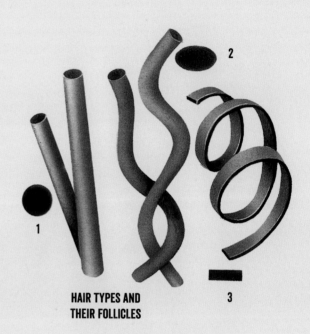

**HAIR TYPES AND THEIR FOLLICLES**

A single hair has a lifespan of around five years.

**FACT FILE**

Most people's hair gradually becomes grey or white as they grow older, because the pigment (called melanin) which gives hair its colour, no longer forms.

# WHERE WOULD YOU FIND FOLLICLES?

You would find follicles at the root of an individual hair. A follicle is a long tunnel that reaches into the lower layers of the skin. At the end of the tiny tunnel, there is a hair papilla. The papilla is where most of the growth takes place, as it is here that nutrients are taken up from the blood.

Slightly below the surface of the skin there are sebaceous glands, which supply the hair with sufficient sebum, the fatty secretion of these glands. A tiny hair-raising muscle is responsible for providing sebum from the sebaceous glands.

## • FACT FILE •

A nail has three parts; the matrix, the plate and the bed. The matrix lies under the surface of the skin at the base of the nail. Most of the matrix is covered by skin.

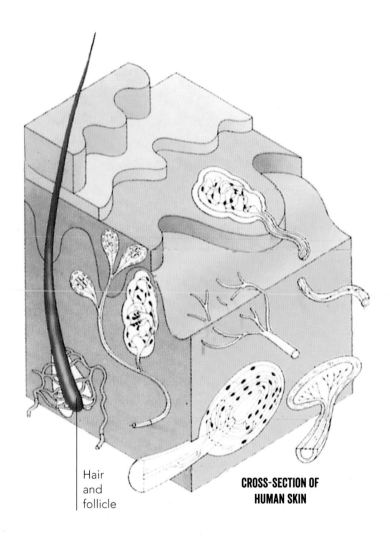

Hair and follicle

**CROSS-SECTION OF HUMAN SKIN**

**?** DID YOU KNOW THAT, AS SOON AS A HAIR IS PLUCKED FROM A FOLLICLE, A NEW ONE STARTS TO GROW IN ITS PLACE.

# WHAT IS SKIN?

Skin covers your body in a pastry-thin layer, in most parts around 2mm thick. It is thicker on the soles of your feet and the palms of your hands, around 3mm.

Skin is both waterproof and stretchy, and it protects you from the outside world by helping to keep out harmful things like dirt and germs.

Skin has two main layers. The protective outer layer is called the epidermis. The skin you can see on your body is the top of the epidermis, which is made up of dead cells. New cells are made at the bottom of the epidermis and gradually push their way upwards.

The inner layer of the skin is called the dermis. The sensory receptors for touch, heat, cold, pressure and pain are here, as well as the nerve-endings that pick up information and carry it to the brain. The dermis is also where sweat is made and hair grows.

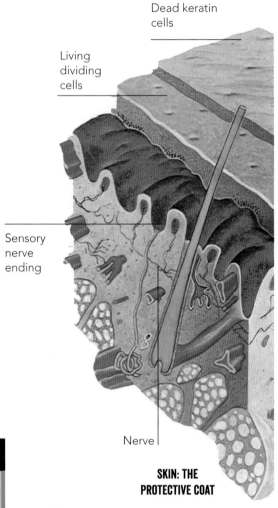

Dead keratin cells

Living dividing cells

Sensory nerve ending

Nerve

**SKIN: THE PROTECTIVE COAT**

## • FACT FILE •

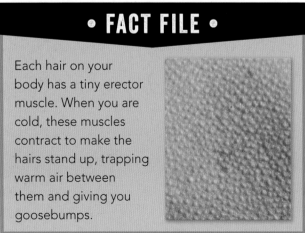

Each hair on your body has a tiny erector muscle. When you are cold, these muscles contract to make the hairs stand up, trapping warm air between them and giving you goosebumps.

**?** DID YOU KNOW THAT A LARGE AMOUNT OF THE DUST IN YOUR HOUSE IS ACTUALLY DEAD SKIN?

# WHAT IS SENSATION?

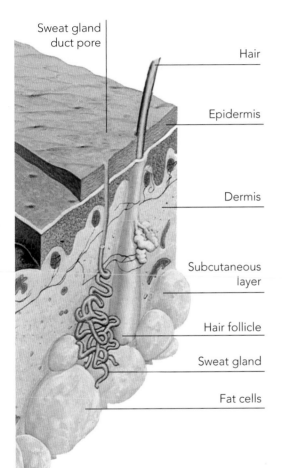

Sweat gland duct pore

Hair

Epidermis

Dermis

Subcutaneous layer

Hair follicle

Sweat gland

Fat cells

Your skin is a huge sense organ with thousands of sensory receptors. Skin receptors are not only sensitive to touch and texture – telling you whether something is smooth or furry, for example. There are also receptors that respond to heat, and ones that respond to cold. Yet others tell you when something is putting pressure on your skin.

Some skin receptors are sensitive to all four. They are called free nerve-endings and they are thought to send out pain signals if messages from touch, heat, cold or pressure receptors are too strong. There are free nerve-endings wrapped around the hairs in your skin, sensitive to each hair's slightest movement. Some areas of the skin are densely packed with nerve endings, as in the finger-tips, while others, as on the back, have comparatively few.

## All mammals have a layer of hair on their skin – even if it is not that easy to see.

# HOW DOES
# SKIN COLOUR DIFFER?

There are certain colour bases in the tissues of the skin called chromogens, which in themselves are colourless. When certain ferments or enzymes act on these colour bases, a definite skin colour results. The base colour of skin is creamy white. A yellow pigment is present in the skin, which is added to the base. Tiny granules of a substance called melanin are also present and although they are brown in colour, when there is a quantity present, they appear to be black.

A further tone is added to the skin by the tinge of red blood circulating in tiny blood vessels. The colour of a person's skin depends on the proportions in which these colours are combined.

Genetics plays a part too, but essentially, all the skin colours of the human race can be obtained by different combinations of these ingredients, which each and every one of us possesses.

**EVERY MINUTE YOUR SKIN SHEDS 30,000 DEAD SKIN CELLS!**

# HOW DO
# FINGERPRINTS DIFFER?

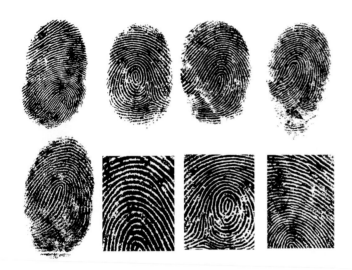

Fingerprints have fascinated people for centuries. They have been used as a method of personal identification since ancient times. But where do fingerprints come from and is it true that they are all different? If you look very closely at a fingerprint, you will notice that it is made up of ridges on the skin. These ridges aren't always continuous; they stop, split into two, form little pockets (called 'lakes') and even appear to cross each other at times. It is these individual features that make the difference between one fingerprint and the next.

Fingerprints are formed before birth, during the development of the hands. Fingerprints are not actually formed in the skin, but are caused by ridges in the flesh underneath the skin. Genetics plays some part in their formation, but even identical twins have different fingerprints. Fingerprints fall into a set number of patterns, which allows us to catalogue them and perform fingerprint searches more easily.

## • FACT FILE •

How do you leave a fingerprint at the scene of a crime? Skin pores produce oils and sweat, which are distributed on your fingers. When you touch something, those liquids are left on the surface, in the shape of your fingerprints.

# GENES
# AND REPRODUCTION

# CONTENTS

# WHAT IS DNA?

DNA is the basic unit of control of human life. It is a highly complex substance formed from a chain of chemical units called nucleotides. All the instructions for growing a new human being are coded into the DNA molecule. It is shaped like a ladder twisted into a spiral. The two long upright strands are joined by a series of rungs of pairs of amino acids, which can only join together in a limited number of ways.

The pattern in which these pairs appear is the code built into the DNA molecule, and groups of these connections form genes. Each DNA molecule is built up of between 100,000 to 10 million atoms. There are 46 chromosomes in the full human set: 23 came from the mother and were in the egg cell, and 23 came from the father in the sperm cell. Every time a cell divides, each piece of DNA in every chromosome is copied.

## • FACT FILE •

A typical DNA molecule is so long and thin that if it were the thickness of spaghetti, it would be 8km (5 miles) long.

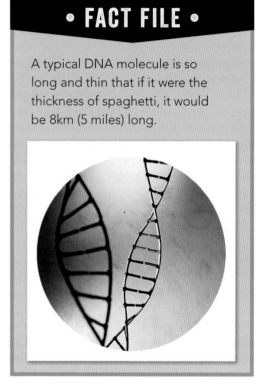

**DNA IS SHORT FOR DEOXYRIBONUCLEIC ACID (THAT'S PRONOUNCED DEE-OX-EE-RYE-BON-NEW-CLAY-IC). TRY IT!**

**HOW A DNA MOLECULE IS FORMED**

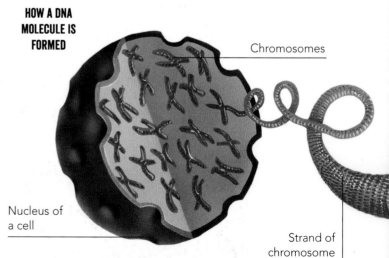

Chromosomes

Nucleus of a cell

Strand of chromosome

# WHY DO WE HAVE CHROMOSOMES?

DNA strands

Pairs of amino acids -

Every cell has a nucleus full of chromosomes. Each one contains thousands of genes, packed with DNA. Each gene has enough information for the production of one protein. This protein may have a small effect within the cell and on the appearance of the body, including skin, eye and hair colour. From the moment of conception the genes issue instructions and every inherited characteristic comes to us via the coding of the genes within the chromosomes.

The Human Genome Project, an international scientific study, cracked the DNA code in 2007. We now understand more fully what makes every individual different, and apply this information in many ways from identifying archaeological remains to predicting reactions to drugs and disease.

**The entire DNA sequence in a single person is referred to as their genome.**

## FACT FILE

Sex chromosomes determine whether the zygote will develop into a boy or a girl. Each body cell contains a pair of sex chromosomes. In females, the two sex chromosomes are identical.

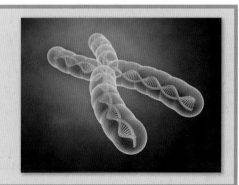

# WHERE IS SPERM PRODUCED?

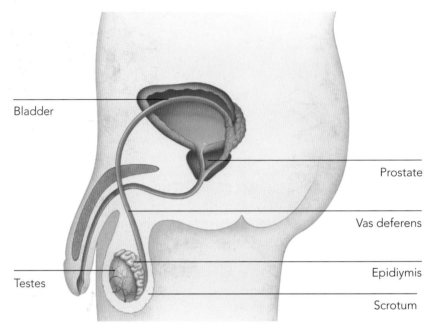

Bladder

Prostate

Vas deferens

Epidiymis

Testes

Scrotum

Sperm, the male sex cells, develop in the testes. It is stored for several days until needed.

The testes contain long tubes called the seminiferous tubules, which are tightly coiled. Sperm is produced continuously in these tubes, then passed to the epididymis and stored in a large duct called the vas deferens. Here, liquid is added to the sperm to make a milky fluid called semen.

Semen is stored in pouches called seminal vesicles. During sexual intercourse the seminal vesicles contract and force out the sperm.

## FACT FILE

Sperms look like tiny tadpoles with rounded heads and long lashing tails. If they are not released they are soon destroyed and replaced.

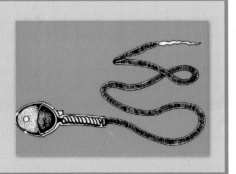

**UP TO 100 MILLION SPERMS ARE PRODUCED EVERY DAY BY THE MALE!**

# WHERE DOES MENSTRUATION TAKE PLACE?

Menstruation, the loss of blood and cells that occurs about once a month in most women of child-bearing age, takes place through the vagina. During each month, blood and cells build up in the lining of a woman's uterus (or womb), a hollow, pear-shaped organ that holds a baby during pregnancy. The thickening of the lining prepares the uterus for pregnancy. If pregnancy does not occur, the lining breaks down. The blood and cells are discharged through the vagina, which is a canal that leads from the uterus to the outside of the body. The process of menstruation lasts from three to seven days, and this period of time is called the menstrual period.

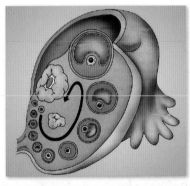

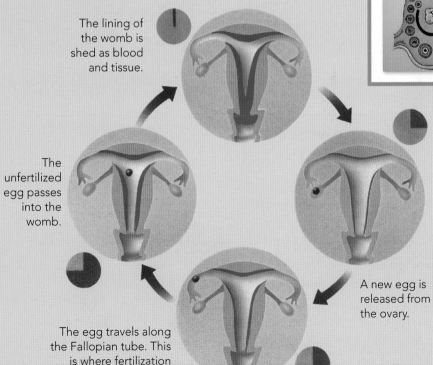

The lining of the womb is shed as blood and tissue.

The unfertilized egg passes into the womb.

The egg travels along the Fallopian tube. This is where fertilization would take place.

A new egg is released from the ovary.

**?**

**DID YOU KNOW THAT A WOMAN IS BORN WITH ALL OF THE EGGS THAT WILL LATER BE RELEASED FROM HER OVARIES?**

# WHAT HAPPENS TO A FERTILIZED EGG?

A fertilized egg (or zygote) goes through a series of changes before it reaches the uterus. Once in the uterus, the zygote develops into a form called the embryo, which develops rapidly.

A zygote travels through the Fallopian tube towards the uterus. Along the way, it begins to divide rapidly into many cells with no increase in overall size. The resulting cell mass is called a morula. By the third or fourth day, the morula enters the uterus

Morula

and the embryo develops from the central cells of the morula. They develop into the placenta, a special organ that enables the embryo to obtain food and oxygen from the mother. After the morula enters the uterus, it continues to divide.

Blastocyst

At this stage, the ball of cells is called a blastocyst. The cells of the blastocyst divide as it floats in the uterus for one or two days. Around the fifth or sixth day of pregnancy, the blastocyst becomes attached to the internal surface of the uterus.

The outer cells of the blastocyst, called the trophoblast, secrete an enzyme that breaks down the lining of the uterus. The trophoblast begins to divide rapidly, invading the uterine tissue. The process of attachment to the uterine wall is called implantation.

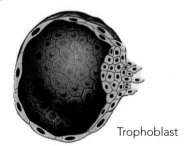

Trophoblast

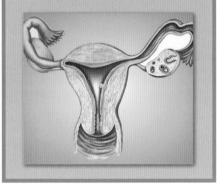

# WHEN ARE TWINS CONCEIVED?

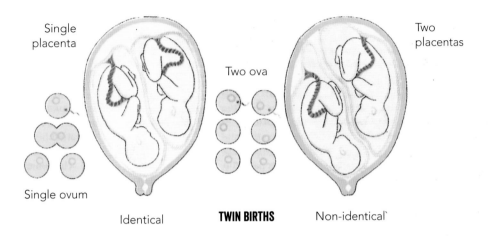

Single placenta

Single ovum

Two ova

Two placentas

Identical

**TWIN BIRTHS**

Non-identical

A baby begins as a fertilized egg – a pinhead-sized egg cell from the mother, which has joined an even smaller tadpole-shaped sperm cell from the father. Although thousands of these sperm cells may cluster around the egg cell, only one of these will fertilize the egg.

Non-identical twins are produced when two eggs are released at the same time, and both are fertilized. They can be the same sex, or brother and sister.

Identical twins are produced when the embryo splits into two in the early stages of its development. This produces two identical children of the same sex. Some identical twins look so alike that they can only be told apart by their fingerprints.

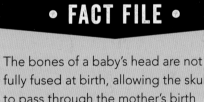

## • FACT FILE •

The bones of a baby's head are not fully fused at birth, allowing the skull to pass through the mother's birth canal. The bones gradually become joined, but a gap at the top of the skull, called the fontanelle, may not close up for several months.

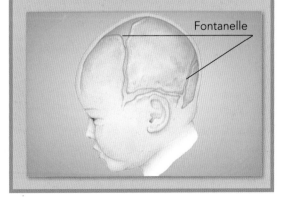

Fontanelle

# WHEN WERE GENES DISCOVERED?

White pea flower in bloom

Genetic engineering is the science of altering the genetic codes deep within our cells. It is hoped that, in future, genetic engineering can be used to cure genetic disorders such as cystic fibrosis by replacing a faulty gene with a properly functioning one.

In the 1800s a monk named Gregor Mendel experimented with characteristics in pea plants by cross-fertilizing plants with different traits. He kept a careful track of the traits displayed by the pea plants produced by cross-fertilization, discovering that the characteristics from the parent plants were inherited by the progeny plants in specific patterns.

Mendel also discovered during his experiments that certain genes seemed more dominant than others. For example, if a pea with a white flower is cross-fertilized with a pea with a pink flower, the resulting flowers will all be pink.

This is obvious in human beings. For example, if a child has a gene for brown eyes from one parent and a gene for blue eyes from the other, the child will always have brown eyes. This is because the gene for brown eyes is a dominant gene.

## • FACT FILE •

Researchers have found important uses for genetic engineering in such fields as medicine, industry and agriculture. Many new uses are predicted for the future.

# WHEN IS A BABY'S GENETIC MAKE-UP DECIDED?

A baby's genetic make-up is fixed from the moment that the egg is fertilized. The division of the nucleus is an essential part of cell division. Each new nucleus contains two sets of genes: one provided by the mother, and the other by the father. Before the cell divides, both sets of genes are copied – termed DNA replication. Each new offspring then receives a full set of genes from each parent.

So it is that every human being inherits some of the characteristics of both parents. This why all kinds of traits, for example, height or curly hair run in families. However, every human being is also a unique individual, subject to the influences of the environment in which he or she grows, the food that is eaten and the illnesses that are caught. These circumstances affect emotional, intellectual and physical development too.

Scientists have debated the contribution that heredity and environment each make to the development of the individual. The Human Genome Project and the decoding of DNA suggest that heredity is more significant than was realized.

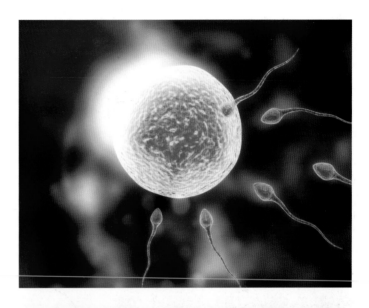

## • FACT FILE •

You may look like your parents, but you are not an exact duplicate of either of them. You inherited half your genes from your father and half from your mother.

# HOW DO WE GET BROWN EYES?

**DOMINANT EYE GENES**

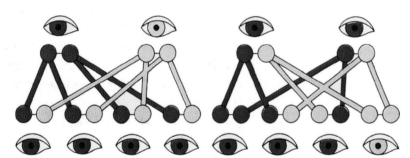

Traits that you inherit from your parents include hair, eye and skin colour, and whether you have lobed or lobeless ears.

At fertilization, the embryo receives genes from both parents. However, not all genes are equal and the 'dominant' genes override the characteristics carried by the rest, which are called 'recessive'.

The gene for brown eyes is always dominant, so if a child receives one gene for blue eyes and one for brown from each parent, the child will always have brown eyes.

It is possible for two brown-eyed parents to have a child with blue eyes if each carries the recessive blue-eyed gene, inherited from their own parents.

# WHERE DOES A BABY DEVELOP?

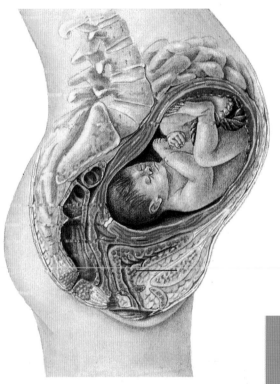

A baby develops in the uterus, or womb – a hollow, muscular organ in the mother's abdomen. The period of development in the uterus lasts about nine months in most cases. During this period, development is more rapid than at any time after birth.

For a baby to develop, a sperm from the father must unite with an egg from the mother. This union of a sperm and an egg is called fertilization. It produces a single cell called a fertilized egg. By a series of remarkable changes, the fertilized egg gradually develops into a baby.

**?** **DID YOU KNOW THAT AN EMBRYO'S HEARTBEAT STARTS SIX WEEKS INTO A MOTHER'S PREGNANCY? A BABY'S LUNGS DEVELOP FROM WEEKS 29 TO 40.**

## FACT FILE

The placenta is an organ composed largely of blood vessels. The placenta is attached to the wall of the uterus. A tubelike structure called the umbilical cord joins the placenta to the embryo at the abdomen. The placenta supplies everything that the embryo needs to live and grow.

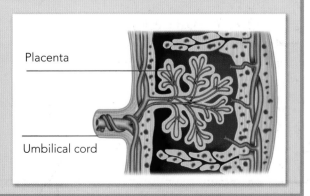

Placenta

Umbilical cord

# WHERE DOES LANUGO FORM ON A FOETUS?

By the fifth month of pregnancy, fine hair called lanugo covers the body of the foetus. Lanugo disappears late in pregnancy or shortly after birth. Hair also appears on the head.

From the ninth week of pregnancy until birth, the developing baby is called a foetus. In the first three months of this period, the foetus increases rapidly in length. It grows about 5cm (2in) in each of these months. In the later months of pregnancy, the most striking change in the foetus is in its weight. Most foetuses gain about 700g (25oz).

The mother can feel movements of the foetus by the fifth month of pregnancy. The eyelids open by the 26th week of pregnancy. By the 28th week, the fingernails and toenails are well developed. Until the 30th week, the foetus appears reddish and transparent because of the thinness of its skin and a lack of fat beneath the skin. In the last six to eight weeks before birth, fat develops rapidly and the foetus becomes smooth and plump.

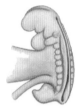 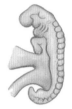

3-week embryo     4-week embryo

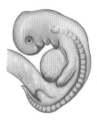 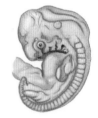

5-week embryo     6-week embryo

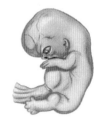 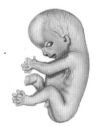

7-week embryo     8-week embryo

## FACT FILE

In most cases, a single egg is fertilized and develops into one baby. Occasionally, however, two or more infants develop and are born at the same time. The birth of more than one baby from the same pregnancy is called multiple birth.

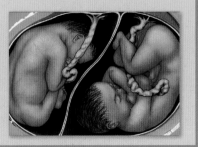

# WHEN ARE BABIES DELIVERED AS A 'BREECH BIRTH'?

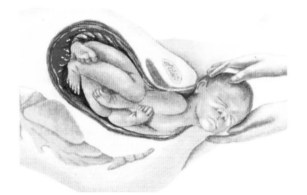

**NORMAL BIRTH**

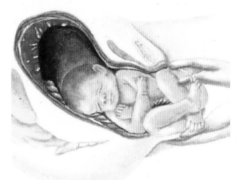

**BREECH BIRTH**

At about 280 days after the baby's inception, the mother starts to feel strong tightening pains, called contractions, in her womb when the birth is near. These contractions become stronger and the neck of the cervix starts to open. As the contractions continue, the baby's head moves down and eventually emerges through the cervix and vagina.

A breech birth is different to a regular birth because the buttocks engage in the pelvis instead of the head. This makes delivery more complicated as the largest part, namely the head, is delivered last.

A breech birth is encountered about once in every thirty deliveries. Because the head in such cases is the last part of the child to be delivered and because this part of the delivery is the most difficult, the umbilical cord may be compressed while the aftercoming head is being born, with the result that the child may be deprived of oxygen.

## • FACT FILE •

Sometimes a baby cannot be born normally through the vagina and so it has to be surgically removed from the mother's womb. This operation is called a caesarean section.

# DAY-TO-DAY
# LIVING

# CONTENTS

# WHAT IS
# INSIDE AN ANIMAL CELL?

All living things, plant and animal, are made from cells. These cells consist mostly of a watery jelly-like material called cytoplasm. Each cell is held together by a very thin flexible membrane, rather like a balloon filled with water. Inside the cell, the cytoplasm is organized into special areas called organelles. These control the functioning of the cell – for example, the production of essential substances called proteins. Tiny organelles called mitochondria use oxygen to break down food and release the energy that powers the cell. An area called the nucleus contains 46 thread-like chromosomes that control the working of the cell. Some cells, such as those lining the intestines, only live for a few days, while other nerve cells within the brain can survive throughout your entire life.

**SCIENTISTS HAVE WORKED OUT THAT AROUND 95 PER CENT OF ALL CELLS IN THE HUMAN BODY ARE BACTERIA!**

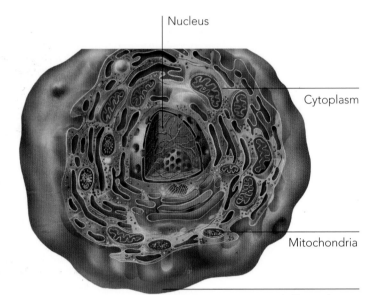

Nucleus

Cytoplasm

Mitochondria

Cell membrane

**THE INSIDE OF A CELL**

The nucleus is the focus point of the cell, containing the genetic information as strands of DNA.

## • FACT FILE •

Cells need food, oxygen and a watery environment in order to survive. Food and water are supplied by the blood and other body fluids, which also carry away waste. Blood contains all of the food substances and chemicals needed by the cell.

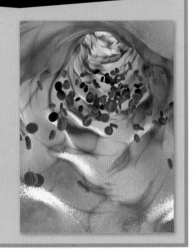

# HOW MANY CELLS DOES THE HUMAN BODY HAVE?

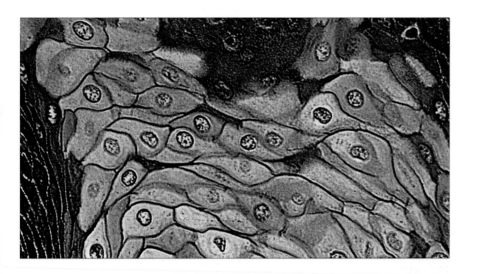

IT WOULD TAKE ABOUT 40,000 OF YOUR RED BLOOD CELLS TO FILL THIS LETTER O!

The human body has more than 10 trillion cells. Written in full, that's 10,000,000,000,000.

A cell is the basic unit of all life and all living things are made up of them.

Most cells are so small they can be seen only with a microscope. It takes millions of cells to make up the skin on the palm of your hand. Some one-celled organisms lead independent lives. Others live in loosely organized groups. As you read these words, for example, nerve cells in your eyes are carrying messages of what you are reading to your brain cells. Muscle cells attached to your eyeballs are moving your eyes across the page.

## • FACT FILE •

All cells have some things in common, whether they are specialized cells or one-celled organisms. A cell is alive – as alive as you are. It 'breathes', takes in food and gets rid of waste. It also grows and reproduces and, in time, it dies.

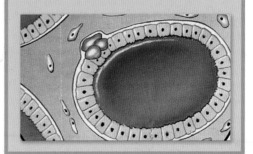

# WHY ARE
# CELLS IMPORTANT?

Lymphocyte

Basophil

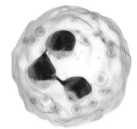

Neutrophil

Eosinophil

Monocyte

**WHITE BLOOD CELLS**

There are five different types of white blood cell, each with its own function, from targetting infections to stalking parasites.

## • FACT FILE •

Metabolism is the term for all of the chemical activity that takes place inside the cells. Metabolism breaks down more complicated substances obtained from food. Our metabolic rate rises during vigorous exercise.

Apart from water, the rest of the body is built from a huge number of complicated chemicals. These chemicals, together with water, are assembled into tiny building blocks called cells. Each cell is self-contained and has a particular function in the body. The shape and appearance of a cell depends on what type of job it has to do. Nerve cells are long and thread-like and can carry messages around the body along the nervous system. Red blood cells are so tiny that they can only be seen under a microscope and are like flattened discs. The sole function of the red blood cell is to combine with oxygen in the lungs and to exchange the oxygen for carbon dioxide in the tissues. White blood cells are shapeless so they can squeeze between other cells and attack invaders such as bacteria. Other cells control the production of essential substances called proteins.

# WHEN DOES MITOSIS OCCUR?

As well as being packed with information, the DNA of chromosomes also has the ability to reproduce itself. Without this, the cells could not pass on information from one generation to the other. The process of cell division in which the cell duplicates itself is called mitosis, which works as follows:

1   The chromosomes become shorter and the nuclear envelope breaks.

2   The chromosomes are released, which duplicate and attach themselves to a cytoplasmic network.

3   The chromosomes are then are drawn apart…

4–7 … to form two new cells with reformed nuclear envelopes.

Mitosis is absolutely essential to life because it provides new cells for growth and for replacement of worn-out cells. Mitosis may take minutes or hours, depending upon the kind of cells and species of organisms. It is influenced by time of day, temperature and chemicals.

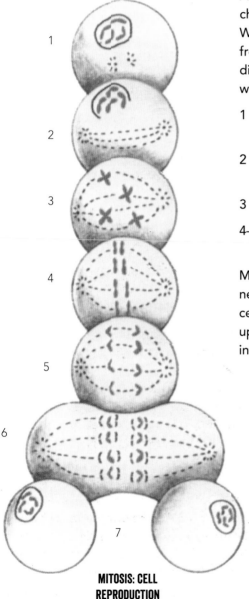

1
2
3
4
5
6
7

**MITOSIS: CELL REPRODUCTION**

## • FACT FILE •

Strictly speaking the term mitosis is used to describe the duplication and distribution of chromosomes – the structures that carry our genetic information.

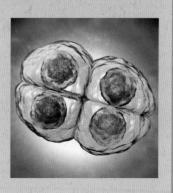

# WHEN DOES THE BODY REPLACE DAMAGED CELLS

The cells in children and young adults are able to repair themselves when damaged. This is not the case in older people, where the process is not as efficient.

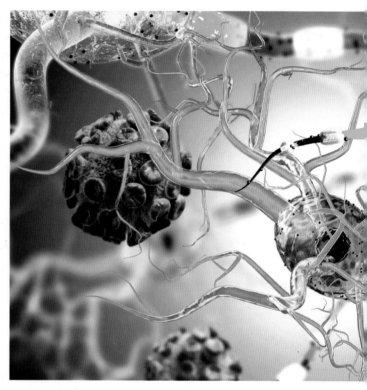

Viruses attacking nerve cells

• **FACT FILE** •

The largest cell in the human body is the egg cell (shown here at zygote stage), which may be fertilized by a sperm cell and grow into a baby.

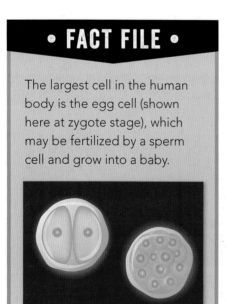

Cells are able to divide very quickly indeed to replace those that are old or have died. Nerve cells are the only ones that cannot be replaced. However, even nerve cells can sometimes grow new connections if the message paths become damaged. Dead and dying cells are removed by white blood cells in the bloodstream, which actually eat them. The liver is also able to break down red blood cells, which are only able to survive for a very short time. The cell's control area, the nucleus, contains all the information and instructions to keep the cells alive and functioning. The information the cell needs is in the form of immensely long coils of chemicals. These structures are known as DNA, which make up the genes.

# WHEN DO CELLS DIE?

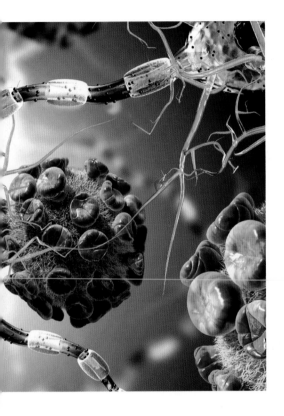

All cells have a fixed lifespan and are replaced automatically as they die off. The more active the cell, the shorter the time it will live. Some white blood cells live for a very short time, and some types that consume dead cells and bacteria survive for only about 30 hours. White cells that fight disease live for two to four years. Cells lining the intestine live for about five days before being replaced.

Below is a list of cell lifespans:

- Skin cells live for 19 days
- Sperm live for 2 months
- Eyelashes live for 3 to 4 months
- Red blood cells live for 4 months
- Liver cells live for 8 months
- Scalp hairs live for 2 to 4 years
- Bone cells live for 15 to 25 years

## FACT FILE

There are three types of nerve cell, each with a different function. Motor neurons control the way your muscles work. Sensory neurons carry messages from your sense organs. Connector neurons pass messages between different parts of the nervous system.

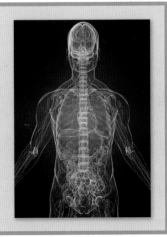

# WHAT ARE A BABY'S DEVELOPMENTAL MILESTONES?

A newborn baby lies with its knees drawn up. It automatically grasps any object that touches its palm and, when held upright, automatically steps as its feet touch something. It roots and sucks the nipple automatically. These reflexes disappear within a few weeks.

At one month old a baby's legs are straighter and by six weeks it can lift its head. The baby sleeps more often than not, but gradually its eyes focus on objects and, at about six weeks, it begins to smile. By six months its birth weight is doubled and the child can sit unaided.

At eight months the preliminary gurglings of speech are heard and the baby can use its thumb. At about ten months it starts to crawl and its birth weight is trebled. The first step may be taken at a year old. The first words may be spoken two or three months later.

## FACT FILE

A baby's personality begins to develop soon after birth. The development continues throughout childhood and even throughout life.

# HOW DOES
# THE BREAST PRODUCE MILK?

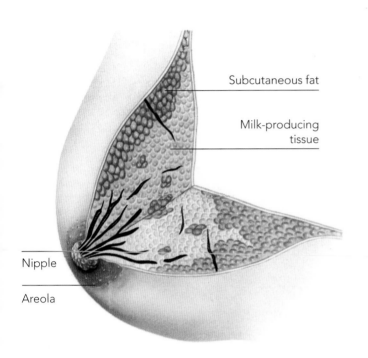

Subcutaneous fat

Milk-producing tissue

Nipple

Areola

Two pituitary hormones are responsible for the production of breast milk: prolactin stimulates the breast to produce milk and oxytocin starts milk flow. The baby's sucking of the nipples also stimulates lactation.

A mother's milk is a complete source of food and energy for the baby. It also contains antibodies that protect the infant from many diseases. The breast is an organ specially designed to produce milk to feed a baby.

Human beings have two breasts, but only those of mature females can produce milk. The breast is composed of 15 to 20 modified sweat glands developing into lobes.

The female breast gland develops rapidly at puberty with secreting cells responding to the hormones in the menstrual cycle. During pregnancy the glands become congested and milk is collected in the lactiferous sinuses, which join behind the areola of the nipple. The areola is lubricated by the moist secretion of sebaceous glands.

## • FACT FILE •

Breast milk is secreted by the lining of the alveoli (right). As the baby feeds, the milk is drawn down the ducts, from where it is sucked out of the nipple.

# HOW DOES YOUR BODY GROW?

The most important forces that cause growth lie inside a living thing from the beginning. These forces are called its heredity. The human body has several stages of growth: embryo and foetus, infant, child, youth, mature adult and old age. People's bodies grow faster in the early weeks of life than at any other time. Even before the end of the first year, they are growing less rapidly. Through the whole period of childhood, they grow at a moderate rate. Then growth starts to speed up again. All human beings are much alike in their growth. But there are important differences. Boys and girls all follow the same general pathway of growth, but each follows it in his or her own way.

4 weeks

8 weeks

12 weeks

**GROWTH STAGES OF A HUMAN FOETUS BEFORE BIRTH**

40 weeks

20 weeks

Newborn babies are fed on their mother's milk, which contains special antibodies, helping to boost the baby's immune system.

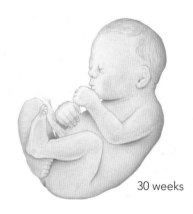

30 weeks

# WHY DO
# WE STOP GROWING?

The average baby is about 51cm (20in) long at birth. Over the next 20 years, humans triple the length of the body they were born with and reach an average height of 175cm (5ft 9in) for a man, 162cm (5ft 3in) for a woman. But why don't we just keep on growing and growing?

In the body there is a system of glands called the endocrine glands which control our growth. The endocrine glands are: the thyroid in the neck, the pituitary attached to the brain, the thymus which is in the chest and the sex glands. The pituitary gland is the one that stimulates our bones to grow. If this works too hard our arms and legs would grow too long and our hands and feet too big. If the gland doesn't work hard enough, we would end up very under-sized.

We continue to grow, but only slightly, after the age of 25, and we reach our maximum height at about the age of 35 or 40. After that, we shrink about half an inch every ten years. The reason for this is the drying-up of the cartilages in our joints and in the spinal column as we get older.

**?**

**DID YOU KNOW THAT THE TALLEST PERSON EVER MEASURED WAS A LOFTY 2.72M (8FT, 11.1IN) TALL?**

## • FACT FILE •

Older people are no longer growing and are often not as active as they used to be. For these reasons they do not need to eat as much and quite often become thinner.

# HOW DO PEOPLE AGE?

Ageing is a result of the gradual failure of the body's cells and organs to replace and repair themselves. This is because there is a limit to the number of times that each cell can divide. As the body's cells begin to near this limit, the rate at which they divide slows down.

Sometimes the new cells that are produced have defects or do not carry out their usual task effectively. Organs can then begin to fail, tissues change in structure, and the chemical reactions that power the body become less efficient. Sometimes the blood supply to the brain is not effective.

The brain cells become starved of oxygen and nutrients, leading to forgetfulness. Strangely, even though recent events may be forgotten, old people often clearly remember events that took place in their childhood.

THE WORLD POPULATION IS GETTING OLDER. SOME ESTIMATES SUGGEST THAT THERE WILL BE 395 MILLION PEOPLE IN THE WORLD AGED 80 OR OVER BY 2050!

## FACT FILE

The skin becomes looser as people age. As skin sags, it forms into wrinkles and creases because the fibres of collagen that normally provide support to the skin become weaker.

# WHEN DO WE SUFFER FROM REFERRED PAIN?

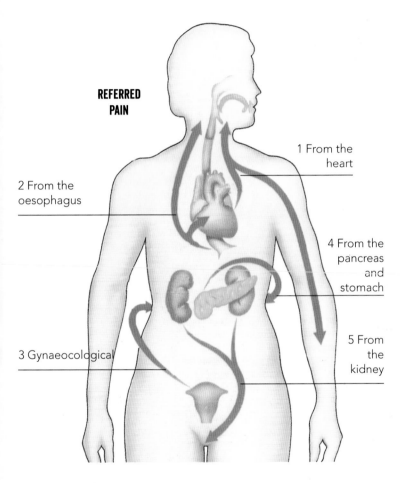

**REFERRED PAIN**

2 From the oesophagus

1 From the heart

4 From the pancreas and stomach

5 From the kidney

3 Gynaeocological

Referred pain is a pain that's source is in one place of the body but we feel it on another part of the body. Internal organs and structure are well supplied with nerves, but pain is widely spread and poorly located compared with skin sensations.

Most of the pain is caused by stretching and contracting, as in the pain of colic. Internal pain will cause stimulation of local nerves in a portion of the spinal cord, and this makes it appear that the pain is coming from the skin, which is supplied by the sensory nerves.

The heart (1) and the oesophagus (2) refer pain to the neck, heart, shoulders and arms. The uterus (3) and pancreas (4) refer pain to the lumber region. The kidneys (5) refer pain into the groin.

Pain from the diaphragm may be referred to the shoulders as the phrenic nerve is formed from the spinal nerves in the neck, which also supply the shoulders.

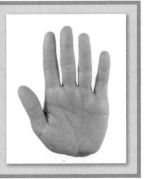

# HOW DO
# WE TALK?

ORGANS OF
SPEECH

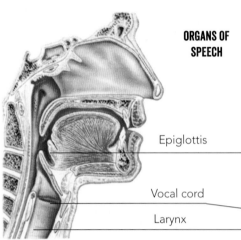

Epiglottis

Vocal cord

Larynx

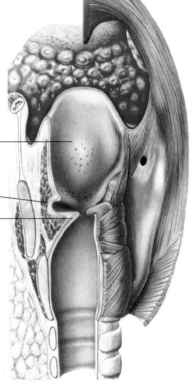

**?**

DID YOU KNOW
THAT MANY OF
THE MUSCLES
THAT YOU USE
FOR TALKING
ALSO COME
INTO USE WHEN
SWALLOWING?

## • FACT FILE •

Although many people
think of speech as our main
way of communicating, we
do not have to use spoken
words. People who can't
speak learn a language
called signing, in which
hands and fingers are used
to signal letters and words.

The sign for love

As air flows out of the lungs, we can use it to make the
sounds of speech and other noises. At the top of the
windpipe, in the sides of the voice box or larynx, are
two stiff, shelf-like folds – called the vocal cords. Criss-
crossed muscles in the voice box can pull them together
so that air passes through a narrow slit between them
and makes them vibrate, creating sounds. As the vocal
cords are pulled tighter, they make higher-pitched
sounds. As the vocal cords loosen, they make lower-
pitched sounds. Of course, when we actually learn to
talk, our speech depends on the development of the
brain and its ability to copy the sounds that we hear.

# WHAT IS
# BODY LANGUAGE?

Body language is the series of gestures and movements we make with our face, head, arms, hands and indeed our whole bodies, to signal thoughts and feelings. Head and facial gestures can say a lot about how we feel. How often do you raise your eyebrows when you are surprised, for instance, or nod your head when you say 'yes'? Our body language shows how we feel. People who are tired tend to hunch up and look smaller. People who are excited and happy make big and confident gestures. Whole body gestures, meaning the way we stand or sit, can also communicate a lot. Confident people tend to show they are sure of themselves by standing up straight.

A fine example of body language is when two dogs meet. You will see them take up a number of different poses at various times – ears and nose down, tail between legs, ears pricked, teeth bared, or tail up and wagging. It is actions like these that allow dogs to tell each other when they want to fight, to run away, or to make friends.

## • FACT FILE •

People's gestures often mean different things in different countries. In some countries people shake hands when they greet each other, for example, but in other countries people rub noses to say hello or goodbye.

DID YOU KNOW THAT THERE ARE SIX UNIVERSAL FACIAL EXPRESSIONS? THEY ARE HAPPINESS, SADNESS, ANGER, DISGUST, FEAR AND SURPRISE.

# HOW DOES
# OUR IMMUNE SYSTEM WORK?

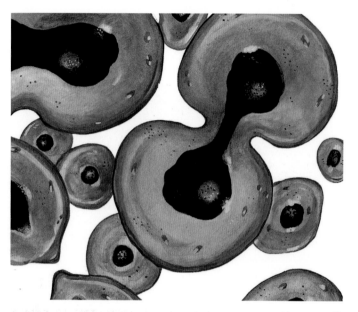

Human cells

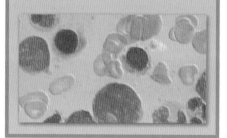
The immune system is a group of cells, molecules and tissues that help defend the body against diseases and other harmful invaders.

The immune system provides protection against a variety of potentially damaging substances that can invade the body. These substances include disease-causing organisms, such as bacteria, fungi, parasites and viruses. The body's ability to resist these invaders is called immunity.

A key feature of the immune system is its ability to destroy foreign invaders while leaving the body's own healthy tissues untouched. Sometimes, however, the immune system attacks and damages these healthy tissues. This reaction is called an autoimmune response or autoimmunity.

**?**

DID YOU KNOW THAT A BAD NIGHT'S SLEEP CAN AFFECT YOUR IMMUNE SYSTEM? NOT SLEEPING WELL CAN REDUCE THE NUMBER OF NATURAL KILLER CELLS IN YOUR BODY, SO WEAKENING THE IMMUNE SYSTEM'S DISEASE-FIGHTING ABILITIES.

# WHAT
# IS LYMPH?

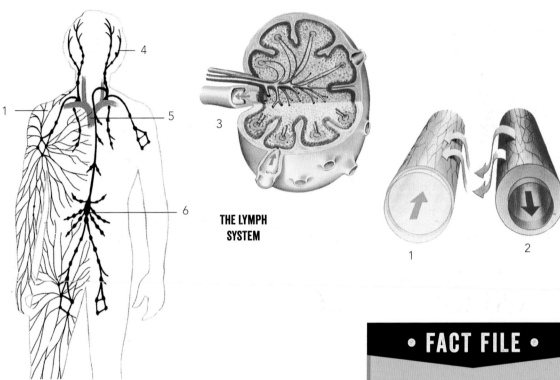

**THE LYMPH SYSTEM**

Your body's main attack force is called the lymph system. Like the blood system, it is a set of vessels that carry liquid round the body. This liquid is called lymph.

Lymph contains special white blood cells called lymphocytes. These can make substances called antibodies, which fight germs and cope with poisons. It works in the following way: The fluid passes out of the capillary (1) and either into the vein or into the smallest, thin-walled lymph vessel (2). These vessels join together to form large channels and finally reach the thoracic duct running next to the descending aorta. This duct joins one of the main branches of the superior vena cava (5). Valves (3) keep lymph flowing in one direction. Lymph glands (4) are found throughout the body and at places where lymph vessels unite (6).

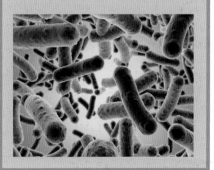

# WHERE ARE
# YOUR ADENOIDS?

The adenoids, also known as pharyngeal tonsils, are a mass of glandlike tissue normally present in the upper part of the throat, directly behind the nasal passages. A small amount of this tissue is always found in the throats of newborn babies.

Usually it shrinks gradually and disappears by the time the child is 10 years old. Sometimes this shrinking process does not take place; instead, the adenoid tissue increases in varying degrees to form a large growth. It is this growth that people commonly call 'adenoids'.

The adenoids form a continuous ring of lymphoid tissue around the back of the throat. If the adenoid tissue causes repeated infections, doctors may remove it in a surgical operation called an adenoidectomy.

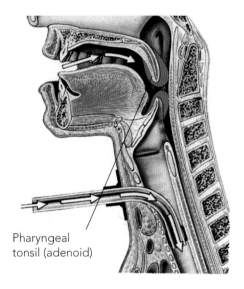

Pharyngeal tonsil (adenoid)

Adenoids tend to grow most when a child is three to five years old, and shrink again between the ages of five to seven.

**FACT FILE**

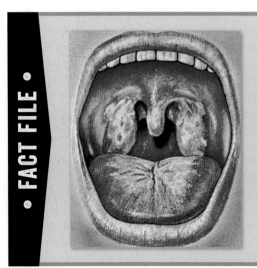

No one really knows the purpose of tonsils, but many medical scientists believe they aid in protecting the respiratory and digestive systems from infection. Tonsils consist of a type of tissue called lymphoid tissue. This tissue produces white blood cells, known as lymphocytes, that help fight infection.

# WHAT DOES
# THE THYROID GLAND DO?

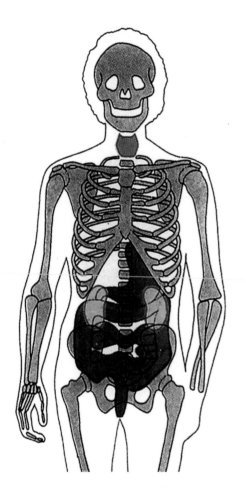

The thyroid gland is a body organ located in the front of the neck. It has two lobes, one on each side of the trachea (or windpipe). The lobes are connected by a thin band of tissue, while a network of blood vessels surrounds the gland. The thyroid takes iodine from the blood and uses it to make the active hormones thyroxine, also called tetraiodothyronine, and triiodothyronine. An inactive form of thyroid hormones is stored inside the lobes in small chambers called follicles.

Thyroid hormones control the body's cell metabolism. When thyroid hormones are released into the bloodstream, cells increase the rate at which they convert oxygen and nutrients into energy and heat for the body's use. During a child's development, thyroid hormones stimulate an increase in growth rate. Release of thyroid hormones also stimulates mental activity and increases the activity of the other hormone-producing glands.

**?**

**DID YOU KNOW THAT THE THYROID GLAND IS USUALLY BIGGER IN WOMEN THAN IT IS IN MEN? IT WEIGHS AROUND 20G (1OZ).**

## FACT FILE

An underactive thyroid, called hypothyroidism, is a defect that results in the low production of thyroid hormones. This deficiency causes an overall decrease in both physical and mental activity.

# WHAT IS AN ALLERGY?

## Up to eight per cent of children in the UK have a food allergy.

An allergy is any condition in which a person reacts in a hypersensitive or unusual manner to any substance or agent. The range of allergies is very broad and people may react to various foods, drugs, dusts, pollens, fabrics, plants, animals, heat, sunlight and many other things.

Whenever a foreign material invades the tissues, the body reacts to fight against it. The body produces certain materials called antibodies, which combine with the foreign material and render it harmless. But should it enter the body a second time, the antibodies are torn away from the body tissues to attack the substance. This causes a chemical substance called histamine to be released, which in turn produce the disorders which are symptoms of an allergy.

### • FACT FILE •

In spring and early summer some people suffer from an allergic reaction to certain plants and pollens. This is called hay fever and can give the symptoms of a heavy cold.

# WHY DO
# SOME PEOPLE GET ASTHMA?

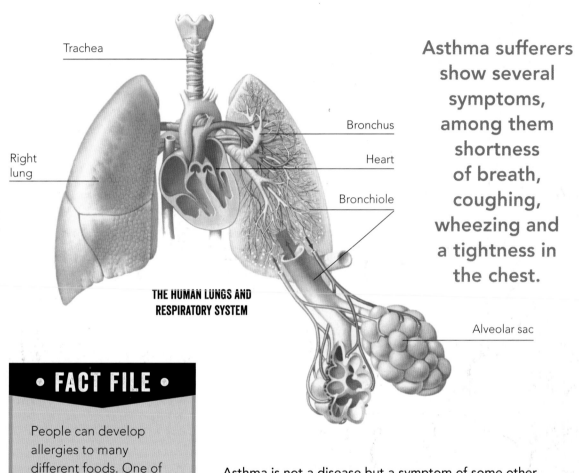

Trachea

Bronchus

Heart

Right lung

Bronchiole

THE HUMAN LUNGS AND
RESPIRATORY SYSTEM

Alveolar sac

Asthma sufferers show several symptoms, among them shortness of breath, coughing, wheezing and a tightness in the chest.

Asthma is not a disease but a symptom of some other condition. When a person suffers from asthma, he or she finds it hard to breathe because there is an obstruction to the flow of air in and out of the lungs. The cause may be an allergy, an emotional disturbance, or atmospheric conditions. If a person develops asthma before he or she is 30 years old, it is usually the result of an allergy. He or she may be sensitive to pollens, dust, animals, or certain foods or medicines.

Children, especially, tend to develop asthma from food allergies. These are often caused by eggs, milk or wheat products. People who have asthma are often put on special diets to eliminate or minimize contact with these foods.

# WHY ARE VIRUSES DIFFERENT FROM BACTERIA?

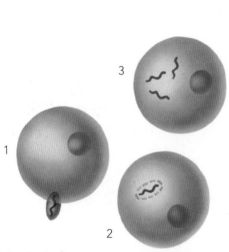

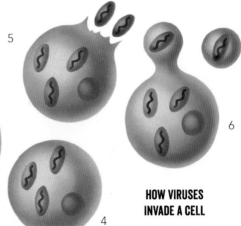

5

3

1

2

4

6

**HOW VIRUSES INVADE A CELL**

Both bacteria and viruses are the most important causes of disease. Bacteria are simple plant-like organisms that can divide very quickly. They cause many common infections such as boils and acne. Viruses are very much smaller and technically they are not alive at all. They can take over the functioning of an infected cell and turn it into a factory producing millions more viruses. Viruses are responsible for many common diseases such as colds and influenza.

The diagram above shows us how viruses invade cells: (1) they shed their outer layer (2) and take over the genetic material in the host cell in order to reproduce themselves (3). They begin to construct protein coats around the new viruses (4) and eventually burst out of the host cell (5) to leave it in an envelope (6) ready to infect new cells.

## • FACT FILE •

Not all bacteria are harmful or disease-causing. Our bodies contain millions of bacteria that break down dead and waste materials. Bacteria in the digestive system aid the digestive process.

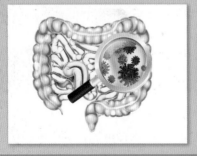

**DID YOU KNOW THAT TRILLIONS OF BACTERIA LIVE IN PERFECT HARMONY IN YOUR DIGESTIVE SYSTEM? THEY ARE REFERRED TO AS GUT FLORA.**

# WHY DO WE TAKE ANTIBIOTICS?

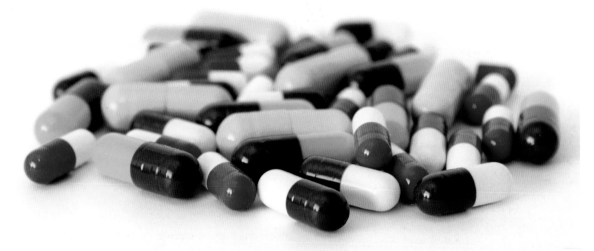

Modern drugs

Antibiotics are chemicals. When these chemicals are put into the body they kill or stop the growth of certain kinds of germs. In other words they help your body to fight off disease.

Many modern antibiotics are made from microbes, which are tiny living things. For example, bacteria and moulds are microbes. The microbes used in making antibiotics are chosen for their ability to produce chemicals that wage war on the microbes of disease. In simple terms this means that man is taking advantage of the struggle that goes on in nature among microbes.

Antibiotics are very effective at curing diseases and work in various ways. One antibiotic may act in different ways against different germs. It may kill the germs in one case and in another only weaken them and let the body's natural defences take over.

## • FACT FILE •

Today a lot of people are turning to natural remedies rather than prescribed drugs. These are made from natural products like roots, plants, flowers and trees.

# WHY IS THE BODY WARM?

In order for the body to carry on its functions efficiently it needs energy. This energy is obtained through a process called combustion. The fuel for this combustion is the food that we take in. The result of combustion in the body is not, of course, a fire or enormous heat. It is a mild, exactly regulated warmth. There are substances in the body whose job it is to combine oxygen with the fuel in an orderly, controlled way.

The body maintains an average temperature regardless of what is going on outside. This is done by the centre in the brain known as the temperature centre, which really consists of three parts: a control centre which regulates the temperature of the blood, one that raises the temperature of the blood when it drops, and a third that cools the blood when the temperature is too high.

**WHEN WE SHIVER IT IS THE BODY'S AUTOMATIC REACTION TO THE TEMPERATURE OF OUR BLOOD DROPPING TOO LOW. SHIVERING ACTUALLY PRODUCES HEAT!**

**• FACT FILE •**

The food we take in is fuel which the body burns up. In this process, about 2,500 calories are being used every day in the body.

# WHY DOES OUR TEMPERATURE RISE WHEN WE'RE ILL?

When the first symptoms of illness appear, the doctor uses a thermometer to check whether the patient has a 'fever'. The average or 'normal' temperature of a healthy body is 37°C (98.6°F). Some diseases make this temperature rise and this high temperature is called a 'fever'.

Fever is in fact a natural response, which helps the body to fight off infection. It makes the vital processes and organs of the body work faster. More hormones are produced as well as enzymes and blood cells, especially the white cells, which attack foreign bacteria and viruses in the bloodstream. The hormones and chemicals have to work much harder when the body is sick. The rate of blood circulation and respiration increases so that the body eliminates toxins and waste more quickly. Perspiration is also increased. It is important, however, to bring down a temperature whilst treating the cause as it can destroy vital protein in the body.

# WHAT IS A CALORIE?

A calorie is a measurement of energy or heat. One calorie is the amount of heat it takes to raise the temperature of one gram of water one degree centigrade. But what does this have to do with food? Well, we eat food to supply us with energy, and so energy in foods is measured in calories. When foods are metabolized – that is, utilized – by being combined with oxygen in the body cells, they give off calories (or energy).

In measuring the energy value of food, we use the 'large' or kilogram calorie, which equals one thousand regular calories. Each type of food, as it 'burns up', furnishes a certain number of calories. For instance, one gram of protein provides four calories, but one gram of fat provides nine calories. The number of calories the body needs depends on the work it has to do.

Pizza, 230 calories per slice

An adult burns around 2,000 calories a day, on average. Any excess calories are stored for later use, usually as body fat.

# HOW MUCH ENERGY DO WE NEED?

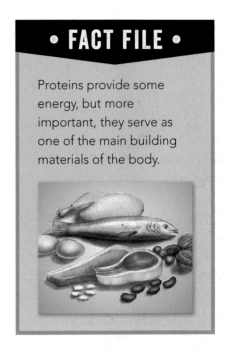
Nutrition is the science that deals with food and how the body uses it. People, like all living things, need food to live. Food supplies the energy for every action we perform, from reading a book to running a race. Food also provides substances that the body needs to build and repair its tissues and to regulate its organs and systems.

The body's need for energy from the diet varies not only with activity, sex, health and climate, but also with age. Humans have different energy requirements for each stage from birth to adulthood. Up to two years old, the rapidly growing child needs more than anyone in proportion to its own size; by old age, when metabolism is slowest, the need is far less. Water is needed in great amounts because the body consists largely of water. Usually, between 50 and 75 per cent of a person's body weight is made up of water.

# WHY DO
# WE NEED VITAMIN C?

The food we take into our bodies supplies us with many important substances such as proteins, fats, carbohydrates, water and mineral substances. But these alone are not enough. In order to maintain life we need other substances known as vitamins. Vitamin C can be found in citrus fruits and fresh vegetables. When there is a lack of vitamins in our body, diseases will occur.

So what actually happens when there is a lack of this vitamin in the body? The blood vessels become fragile and bleed easily. Black-and-blue marks appear on the skin and near the eyes. The gums bleed easily. Our hormones and enzymes do not function well and our resistance to infection by bacteria is lowered.

Before we knew about vitamins, it had been observed that when people couldn't get certain foods, diseases would develop. Sailors, for instance, who went on long trips and couldn't get fresh vegetables, would develop a disease called scurvy. In the 17th century British sailors were given lemons and limes to prevent this disease.

## • FACT FILE •

Fruits contain energy and a range of essential vitamins and minerals. Vitamins are chemicals that we need in order to stay healthy. Some are stored in the body, others need to be eaten every day.

# WHY ARE **CARBOHYDRATES** IMPORTANT?

Carbohydrates should account for at least 50 per cent of the calories in your diet – that is around 300g (11oz) of carbohydrates for an adult.

Human beings need a certain amount of food each day to supply them with energy. Almost all foods can supply some energy, but carbohydrates give us the most.

Carbohydrates include foods like bread, cereal, potatoes, rice, noodles and pasta. Our bodies have other requirements as well. In order to make sure that we are taking in everything we need, we should eat a wide variety of foods, with the correct amounts of carbohydrates, fat and protein.

A diet that fulfils these requirements is called a balanced diet. These food groups serve different purposes: carbohydrates for energy, protein to build and repair cells and to keep our bones, muscles, blood and skin at their optimum health.

## • FACT FILE •

Bananas are a very good source of energy as the body absorbs them very quickly. Ripe bananas give off a gas that causes other fruit to ripen rapidly and then rot.

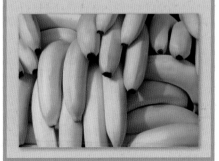

# HOW CAN ENZYMES HELP US?

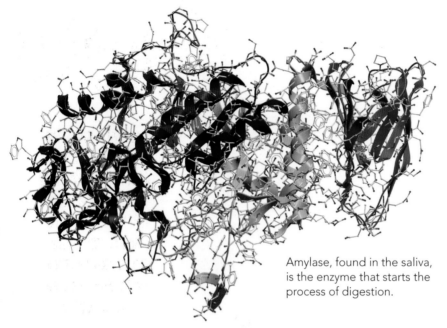

Amylase, found in the saliva, is the enzyme that starts the process of digestion.

**WITHOUT ENZYMES, A PERSON COULD NOT BREATHE, SEE, MOVE OR DIGEST FOOD!**

An enzyme is a molecule that speeds up chemical reactions in all living things. Without enzymes, these reactions would occur too slowly or not at all, and no life would be possible. The human body has thousands of kinds of enzymes. Each kind does one specific job. Enzymes have many uses in addition to their natural functions in the body. Manufacturers use enzymes in making a wide variety of products. Some detergents contain enzymes that break down protein or fats that cause stains. Enzymes are also used in the manufacture of antibiotics, beer, bread, cheese, coffee, sugars, vinegar, vitamins and many other products. Physicians use medicines containing enzymes to help clean wounds, dissolve blood clots, relieve certain forms of leukaemia and check allergic reactions to penicillin. Doctors also diagnose some diseases by measuring the amount of various enzymes in blood and other body fluids. Such diseases include anaemia, cancer, leukaemia and heart and liver ailments.

## • FACT FILE •

In the future, enzymes may be widely used to change raw sewage into useful products. Enzymes may also be used to help get rid of spilled oil that harms lakes and oceans. The enzymes would turn the oil into food for sea plants.

# WHY IS EXERCISE GOOD FOR US?

Regular exercise is important because it keeps bones, joints and muscles healthy. During any physical exertion, the rate at which the heart beats increases, as it pumps more oxygenated blood around the body. How quickly the heart rate returns to normal after exercise is one way to assess how fit someone is and how exercise is actually improving their fitness.

There was a time when almost everyone did manual work of some kind. It was essential for survival. Human bodies were not designed for the inactive lives many of us now lead. That is why exercise is important for good health.

### • FACT FILE •

Swimming is a very good form of exercise as it uses lots of muscles without causing strain.

# WHY IS
# WATER GOOD FOR US?

Water is absolutely essential to every single life form. Every living cell – in plants and animals alike – depends on this substance because cells, the basic units that make up all living things, contain water molecules without which these basic units would be very different and of no use.

Human beings can go without food for a considerable time but without drinking fresh water we would die very quickly. During a 24-hour period, an adult human being takes in about 1.90 litres (3⅓pt) of water as fluids and 0.95 litres (1½pt) in so-called solid foods, such as fruit, vegetables, bread and meat. Since these foods are also made up of cells they are not really dry but are indeed 30–90 per cent water. In addition to this 2.85 litres (5pt) that are taken in, about 9.5 litres (17pt) of water pass back and forth within the body between the various organ systems. There are about 4.75 litres (8⅓pt) of blood in the vessels of the body and 2.85 litres (5pt) of this is water. The blood cannot be diluted.

**?**

**DID YOU KNOW THAT MORE THAN HALF THE HUMAN BODY IS MADE UP OF WATER? MUCH THE SAME IS TRUE OF ALL OTHER LIVING THINGS.**

**• FACT FILE •**

Our sense of thirst is controlled by the brain. When the body requires more water, we experience the sensation of thirst. Usually our mouth and throat become dry – a signal for us to drink more fluids.

# WHY DO
# WE PERSPIRE?

Perspiration is one of the ways in which the body is kept at a normal temperature, around 37°C (98.6°F).

If we are too hot the vessels in the skin are opened so that the extra heat can radiate away and also to help our perspiration to evaporate.

Perspiration is like a shower that washes the body out from within. The fluid flows out through millions of tiny openings in the skin in the form of microscopic drops. These drops evaporate quickly and cool the body when necessary.

## • FACT FILE •

Perspiration is the body's own way of cooling down quickly. When a liquid evaporates it takes heat from wherever it is located.

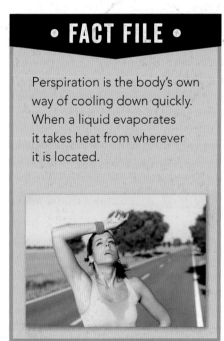

**AN ADULT HUMAN HAS MORE THAN TWO MILLION SWEAT GLANDS ON HIS OR HER BODY. THE HIGHEST CONCENTRATION OF THESE IS ON THE FEET!**

# PICTURE CREDITS

**Images supplied by Dreamstime**

icons: Brain (5, 6–25) Carla F. Castagno; Joint (5, 26–51), Ear (5, 96–115), Tooth (5, 116–127) Alexandragl; Heart (5, 52–75), Stomach (5, 76–95), DNA (5, 128–141) Alexander Ryabintsev; Human Body (5, 142–175) Vectoronly; Hand (throughout) Selman Amer.

8t, 30r, 31t Oguzaral; 8b Kenishirotie; 9t, 88t Guniita; 9b, 90b Elena Elisseeva; 10t Skypixel; 10b Danilo Sanino; 11b Valentyn75; 13b Milan Martaus; 15t, 43t, 51r, 62br, 63t, 85t, 149b Sebastian Kaulitzki; 16b Gstockstudio1; 17b Fizkes; 18–19t Dmitroscope; 18b Anna Khomulo; 19r Danhughes; 20–21t Iodrakon; 20b Jaye Thompson; 21b Goncharuk Maksym; 22l, 23t, 104b Pavla Zakova; 22r John Takai; 24l Timhope; 25l Woraphon Banchobdi; 25r 3dalia; 28l Barbara Helgason; 29b Ocskay Bence; 30l Alexonline; 31b, 122b Absolut_photos; 33b Andres Rodriguez; 37t Kurhan; 38t Itsmejust; 38b Zoya Fedorova; 39t Alila07; 39b Kameel4u; 40b Jacek Chabraszewski; 42b Science Pics; 43b Arkadi Bojaršinov; 47b Ron Chapple; 48b Saintho; 49l Val_th; 49rJosha42; 56b Wavebreakmedia Ltd; 57b Andrei Malov; 58/59t Rob3000; 59b Martinmark; 65b Levente Gyori; 67l Monika Wisniewska; 67r Nathan Allred; 70b Jppi_stu; 73l Irina Mazovka; 73r Razvan Ionut Dragomirescu; 74tRob3000; 74b Raja Rc; 75t Coxie555; 75b Ssuaphoto; 79t, 137b, 153r Monkey Business Images; 82b Mkkans; 86b Plmrue; 87l Alila07; 89t, 148b Designua; 90t Terriana; 91t, 139b Alexluengo; 91b roblan; 100b Christopher Dodge; 101b Pavel Losevsky; 102b Norman Bateman; 103b Szerdahelyi Adam; 105l Jason Stitt; 105r Marcelo Poleze; 106b Fotoeye75; 110b Monika Wisniewska; 111b Annashepulova; 112b Leo Lintang; 113t Gaurav Masand; 113b Andrey Kiselev; 114b James Steidl; 115b Igor Stepovik; 118b Mytime; 119t Kopitoto; 119b Chris Curtis; 129b Funkipics; 121tl Goodluz; 121tr Suzanne Tucker; 121b Andres Rodriguez; ; 124b Tyler Olson; 125b, 173b Anke Van Wyk; 126l Boggy; 126r Noblige; 127t Andy Brown; 127b Rolffimages; 131b Sashkinw; 136t Nicolae Gherasim; 136b Lawrence Wee; 137t Abhijith Ar; 138b Michael Biehler; 141b Jeffrey Williams; 144b Vampy1; 146t Decade3d; 146b Empipe; 147b Ilexx; 148/149t Ralwel; 150t Dml5050; 150b Joellen Armstrong; 152b Evgenyatamanenko; 153l Andreblais; 154t Brett Critchley; 154b Richlyons; 155b Gradts; 156b Sparkia; 157t Creativefire; 157b Lasto4ka81; 159b Guido Vrola; 162t Catalina Zaharescu Tiensuu; 162b Glazyuk; 163b Okea; 164b Christos Georghiou; 165t Hannu Viitanen; 165b Martina Osmy; 166/167t Marzanna Syncerz; 166b Robyn Mackenzie; 168/169t Taiga; 170t; Andersastphoto; 170b Charlotte Leaper; 171b Evgenia82; 171b Baloncici; 172t Leonid Andronov; 172b Sebastianknight; 173t Jennifer Russell; 174/175t Luchschen; p174b Danil Chepko; 175b Dirima.

**All other images copyright © Octopus Publishing Group Ltd**